Jacob Abbott

Rollo on the Rhine

Jacob Abbott

Rollo on the Rhine

ISBN/EAN: 9783337375744

Printed in Europe, USA, Canada, Australia, Japan

Cover: Foto ©Andreas Hilbeck / pixelio.de

More available books at **www.hansebooks.com**

ROLLO ON THE RHINE,

BY

JACOB ABBOTT.

NEW YORK:
SHELDON & CO., 667 BROADWAY
AND 214 & 216 MERCER ST.,
GRAND CENTRAL HOTEL.

PRINCIPAL PERSONS OF THE STORY.

ROLLO ; twelve years of age.

MR. and MRS. HOLIDAY ; Rollo's father and mother, travelling in Europe.

THANNY ; Rollo's younger brother.

JANE ; Rollo's cousin, adopted by Mr. and Mrs. Holiday.

MR. GEORGE ; a young gentleman, Rollo's uncle.

CONTENTS.

ENGRAVINGS.

RIDE. — See chap. 12.

ROLLO ON THE RHINE.

CHAPTER I

THE APPROACH TO COLOGNE.

A birdseye view of Europe.	Switzerland ; Tyrol ; Savoy.

IF a man were to be raised in a balloon high enough above the continent of Europe to survey the whole of it at one view, he would see the land gradually rising from the borders of the sea on every side, towards a portion near the centre, where he would behold a vast region of mountainous country, with torrents of water running down the slopes and through the valleys of it, while the summits were tipped with perpetual snow. The central part of this mass of mountains forms what is called Switzerland, the eastern part is the Tyrol, and the western Savoy. But though the men who live on these mountains have thus made three countries out of them, the whole region is in nature one. It constitutes one mighty mass of mountainous land, which is lifted up so high into the air that all the summits rise into the regions of intense and perpetual cold, and so condense continually, from the atmosphere, inexhaustible quantities of rain and snow.

The water which falls upon this mountainous region must of course find its way to the sea. In doing so the thousands of smaller torrents unite with each other into larger and larger streams, until at length they make four mighty rivers — the largest and most celebrated in Europe. All the streams of the southern slopes of the mountains form one great river, which flows east into the Adriatic. This river is the Po. On the western side the thousands of mountain torrents combine and form the Rhone, which, making a great bend, turns to the southward, and flows into the Mediterranean. On the eastern side the water can find no escape till it has traversed the whole continent to the eastward, and reached the Black Sea. This stream is the Danube. And finally, on the north the immense number of cascades and torrents which come out from the glaciers, or pour down the ravines, or meander through the valleys, or issue from the lakes, of the northern slope of the mountains, combine at Basle, and flow north across the whole continent, nearly six hundred miles, to the North Sea. This river is the Rhine.

All this, which I have thus been explaining,

may be seen very clearly if you turn to any map
of Europe, and find the mountainous region in the
centre, and then trace the courses of the four
great rivers, as I have described them.

It would seem that the country through which
the River Rhine now flows was at first very un-
even, presenting valleys and broad depressions,
which the waters of the river filled, thus forming
great shallow lakes, that extended over very considerable tracts of country. In process of time,
however, these lakes became filled with the sedi-
ment which was brought down by the river, and
thus great flat plains of very rich and level land
were formed. At every inundation of the river,
of course, these plains, or intervals, as they are
sometimes called, would be overflowed, and fresh
deposits would be laid upon them ; so that in the
course of ages the surface of them would rise
several feet above the ordinary level of the river.
In fact they would continue to rise in this way
until they were out of the reach of the highest
inundations.

Immense plains of the most fertile land, which
seem to have been formed in this way, exist at
the present time along the banks of the Rhine at
various places. These plains are all very highly
cultivated, and are rich and beautiful beyond description. To see them, however, it is necessary

to travel over them in a diligence, or post chaise,
or by railway trains ; for in sailing up and down
the river, along the margin of them, in a steamboat, you are not high enough to overlook them.
You see nothing all the way, in these places, but
a low, green bank on each side of the river, with
a fringe of trees and shrubbery along the margin
of it.

For about one hundred miles of its course,
however, near the central portion of it, the river
flows through a very wild and mountainous district of country, or rather through a district
which was once wild, though now, even in the
steepest slopes and declivities, it is cultivated like
a garden. The reason why these mountainous
regions are so highly cultivated is because the
soil and climate are such that they produce the
best and most delicious grapes in the world.
They have consequently, from time immemorial,
been inhabited by a dense population. Every
foot of ground where there is room for a vine to
grow is valuable, and where the slope was originally steep and rocky, the peasants of former
ages have gathered out the rocks and stones, and
built walls of them to terrace up the land. The
villages of these peasants, too, are seen every
where nestling in the valleys, and clinging to the
sides of the hills, while the summits of almost all

the elevations are crowned with the ruins of old feudal castles built by barons, or chiefs, or kings, or military bishops of ancient times, famous in history. This picturesque portion of the river, which extends from Bonn, a little above Cologne, to Mayence, — which towns you will readily find on almost any map of Europe, — was the part which Mr. George and Rollo particularly desired to see. When they left Switzerland they intended to come down the river, and see the scenery in descending. But Mr. George met some friends of his on the frontier, who persuaded him to make a short tour with them in Germany, and so come to the Rhine at Cologne.

"We can then," said he to Rollo, "go *up* the river, and see it in ascending, which I think is the best way. When we get through all the fine scenery, — which we shall do at Mayence, — we can then go up to Strasbourg, and take the railroad there for Paris — the same way that we came."

"Yes," said Rollo, "I shall like that."

Rollo liked it simply because it would make the journey longer.

When at length, at the end of the tour in Germany, our travellers were approaching Cologne on the Rhine, Rollo began to look out, some miles before they reached it, to watch for the first appearance of the town. He had been riding in

the coupé of the diligence* with his uncle; but
now, in order that he might see better, he had
changed his place, and taken a seat on the banquette.   The banquette is a seat on the top of
the coach, and though it is covered above, it is
open in front, and so it affords an excellent view.
Mr. George remained in the coupé, being very
much interested in reading his guide book.

At length Rollo called out to tell his uncle
that the city was in view.   The windows of the
coupé were open, so that by leaning over and
looking down he could speak to his uncle without
any difficulty.

Mr. George was so busy reading his guide
book that he paid little attention to what Rollo
said.

"Uncle George," said Rollo, calling louder,
"I can see the city; and in the midst of it is a
church with a great square tower, and something
very singular on the top of it."

Mr. George still continued his reading.

"There is a spire on the top of the church,"
continued Rollo, "but it is bent down on one
side entirely, as if it had half blown over."

"O, no," said Mr. George, still continuing to
read.

* The stage coaches on the continent of Europe are called
diligences.

Viewing Cologne from the diligence.

"It really is," said Rollo. "I wish you would look, uncle George. It is something very singular indeed."

COLOGNE IN SIGHT.

Mr. George yielded at length to these importunities, and looked out. The country around in every direction was one vast plain, covered with fields of grain, luxuriant and beautiful beyond

20   ROLLO ON THE RHINE.

Singular appearance of the fields.   Rollo's companion.

description. It was without any fences or other divisions except such as were produced by different kinds of cultivation, so that the view extended interminably in almost every direction. There were rows and copses of trees here and there, giving variety and life to the view, and from among them were sometimes to be seen the spires of distant villages. In the distance, too, in the direction in which Rollo pointed, lay the town of Cologne. The roofs of the houses extended over a very wide area, and among them there was seen a dark square tower, very high, and crowned, as Rollo had said, with what seemed to be a spire, only it was bent over half way; and there it lay at an angle at which no spire could possibly stand.

"What can it mean?" asked Rollo.

"I am sure I do not know," said Mr. George.

Next to Rollo, on the banquette, was seated a young man, who had mounted up there about an hour before, though Rollo had not yet spoken to him. Rollo now, however, turned to him, and asked him, in English, if he spoke English.

The young man smiled and shook his head, implying that he did not understand.

Rollo then asked him, in French, if he spoke French.

The young man said, "*Nein.*" *

* Pronounced *nine*

Rollo knew that *nein* was the German word for *no*, and he presumed that the language of his fellow-traveller was German. So he pointed to the steeple, and asked, —

" *Was ist das ?* "

This phrase, *Was* * *ist das ?* is the German of What is that? Rollo knew very little of German, but he had learned this question long before, having had occasion to ask it a great many times. It is true he seldom or never could understand the answers he got to it, but that did not prevent him from asking it continually whenever there was occasion. He said it was some satisfaction to find that the people could understand his question, even if he could not understand what they said in reply to it.

The man immediately commenced an earnest explanation ; but Rollo could not understand one word of it, from beginning to end.

The truth of the case was, that the supposed leaning spire, which Rollo saw, was in reality a monstrous *crane* that was mounted on one of the towers of the celebrated unfinished cathedral at Cologne. This cathedral was commenced about six hundred years ago, and was meant to be the grandest edifice of the kind in the world. They laid out the plan of it five hu‾dred feet long, and

---

* The *w* is pronounced like *v*.

two hundred and fifty feet wide, and designed to carry up the towers and spires five hundred feet high. You can see now how long this church was to be by going out into the road, or to any other smooth and level place, and there measuring off two hundred and fifty paces by walking. The pace — that is, the *long step* — of a boy of ten or twelve years old is probably about two feet. That of a full grown man is reckoned at three feet. So that by walking off, *by long steps*, till you have counted two hundred and fifty of them, you can see how long this church was to be ; and then by turning a corner and measuring one hundred and twenty-five paces in a line at right angles to the first, you will see how wide it was to be. To walk entirely round such an area as this would be nearly a third of a mile.

The church was laid out and begun, and during the whole generation of the workmen that began it, the building was prosecuted with all the means and money that could be procured ; and when that generation passed away, the next continued the work, until, at length, in about a hundred years it was so far advanced that a portion of it could have a roof put over it, and be consecrated as a church. They still went on, for one or two centuries more, until they had carried up the walls to a considerable height in many parts, and

The building is interrupted.

had raised one of the towers to an elevation of about a hundred and fifty feet. When the work had advanced thus far the government of Holland, in the course of some of the wars in which they were engaged, closed the mouth of the Rhine, so that the ships of Cologne could no more go up and down to get out to sea. This they could easily do, for the country of Holland is situated at the mouth of the Rhine, and the Dutch government was at that time extremely powerful. They had strong fleets and great fortresses at the mouth of the river, and thus they could easily control the navigation of it. Thus the merchants of Cologne could no more import goods from foreign lands for other people to come there and buy, but the inhabitants were obliged to send to Holland to purchase what they required for themselves. The town, therefore, declined greatly in wealth and prosperity, and no more money could be raised for carrying on the work of the cathedral.

At the time when the work was interrupted the builders were engaged chiefly on one of the towers, which they had carried up about one hundred and fifty feet. The stones which were used for this tower were very large, and in order to hoist them up the workmen used a monstrous crane, which was reared on the summit of it.

This crane was made of timbers rising obliquely from a revolving platform in the centre, and meeting in a point which projected beyond the wall in such a manner that a chain from the end of it, hanging freely, would descend to the ground. The stones which were to go up were then fastened to this chain, and hoisted up by machinery. When they were raised high enough, that is, just above the edge of the wall, the whole crane was turned round upon its platform, in such a manner as to bring the stone in over the wall; and then it was let down into the place which had been prepared to receive it.

When the work on the cathedral was suspended on account of the want of funds, the men left this crane on the top of the tower, because they hoped to be able to resume the work again before long. But years and generations passed, and the prospect did not mend; and at last the old crane, which in its lofty position was exposed to all the storms and tempests of the sky, of course began gradually to decay. It is true it was protected as much as possible by a sort of casing made around it, to shelter it from the weather; but notwithstanding this, in the course of several centuries it became so unsound that there began to be danger that it might fall. The authorities of the town, therefore, decided to take

The crane taken down.	The thunder storm.	A new crane.

it down, intending to postpone putting up a new
one until the work of finishing the cathedral
should be resumed, if indeed it ever should be
resumed.

The people of the town were very sorry to see
the crane taken down. It had stood there, like
a leaning spire, upon the top of the cathedral,
from their earliest childhood, and from the earliest childhood, in fact, of their fathers and grand-
fathers before them. Besides, the taking down of
the crane seemed to be, in some sense, an indica-
tion that the thought of ever finishing the cathedral was abandoned. This made them still more
uneasy, and a short time afterwards a tremendous
thunder storm occurred, and this the people con-
sidered as an expression of the displeasure of
Heaven at the impiety of forsaking such a work,
and as a warning to them to put up the crane
again. So a new crane was made, and mounted
on the tower as before, and being encased and
enclosed like the other, it had at a distance the
appearance of a leaning spire, and it was this
which had attracted Rollo's attention in his ap-
proach to Cologne.

Within a few years, on account of the opening
again of the navigation of the Rhine, and other
causes, the city of Cologne, with all the surrounding country, has been returning to its former

prosperity, and the plan of finishing the cathedral has been resumed. The government of Prussia takes a great interest in the undertaking, and the kings and princes of other countries in Germany make contributions to it. A society has been organized, too, to collect funds for this purpose all over Europe. More than a million of dollars have already been raised, and the work of completing the cathedral has been resumed in good earnest, and is now rapidly going on.

All this Rollo's fellow-traveller attempted to explain to him ; but as he spoke in German, Rollo did not understand him.

When Mr. George and Rollo reached their hotel, and had got fairly established in their room, Mr. George took his cane and prepared to "go exploring," as he called it.

" Well, Rollo," said he, " what shall we go to see first ? "

" I want to go and see the cathedral," replied Rollo.

" The cathedral ? " said Mr. George. "I am surprised at that. You don't usually care much about churches."

" But this does not look much like a church," said Rollo. " I saw the end of it as we came into the town. It looks like a range of cliffs rising high into the air, with grass and bushes growing on the top of them, and wolves and bears reaching out their heads and looking down."

Mr. George complied with Rollo's request, and went to see the cathedral first. The adventures which the travellers met with on the excursion will be described in the next chapter.

CHAPTER II.

THE UNFINISHED CATHEDRAL.

As soon as Mr. George and Rollo issued from the door of their hotel into the street, which was very narrow and without sidewalks, so that they were obliged to walk in the middle of it, a young man, plainly but neatly dressed, came up to them from behind, and said something to them in German. He was what is called a commissioner, and he was coming to offer to act as their guide in seeing the town.

Nearly all the travelling on the Rhine is *pleasure* travelling. The strangers consequently, who arrive at any town or city by the steamboats and by railway, come, almost all of them, for the purpose of seeing the churches and castles, and other wonders of the place, and not to transact business; and in every town there is a great number of persons whose employment it is to act as guides in showing these things. These men hover about the doors of the hotels, and gather in front of all the celebrated churches, and in all public places where travellers are expected to go ; and as soon as they see a gentleman, or a party of gentlemen and ladies, coming out of their hotel, or approaching any place of public interest, they immediately come up to them, and offer their services. Sometimes their services are valuable, and the traveller is very ready to avail himself of them, especially when in any particular town there is a great deal to see, and he has but little time to see it. At other times, however, it is much pleasanter to go alone to the remarkable places, as a map of the city will enable any one to find them very easily, and the guide book explains them in a much more satisfactory manner than any of these commissioners can do it.

The commissioners generally speak French, English, and German, and after trying one of these tongues upon the strangers whom they accost, and finding that they are not understood, they try another and another until they succeed.

The commissioner in this case addressed Mr. George first in German. Mr. George said, "*Nein*," meaning no, and walked on.

The commissioner followed by his side, and began to talk in French, enumerating the various churches and other objects of interest in Cologue, and offering to go and show them.

" No," said Mr. George, " I am acquainted with the town, and I have no need of a guide."

Mr. George had studied the map and the guide book, until he knew the town quite well enough for all his purposes.

" You speak English, perhaps," said the commissioner, and then proceeded to repeat what he had said before, in broken English. He supposed that Mr. George and Rollo were English people, and that they would be more likely to engage him as a guide, if they found that he could explain the wonders to them in their own language.

Mr. George said, " No, no, I do not wish for a guide."

" Dere is die churts of St. Ursula," said the commissioner, persisting, " and die grand towers of die gross St. Martin, which is rare bu'ful."

Mr. George finding that refusals did no good, determined to take no further notice of the commissioner, and so began to talk to Rollo, walking on all the time. The commissioner continued for some time to enumerate the churches and other public buildings, which he could show the strangers if they would but put themselves under his guidance ; but when at length he found that they would not listen to him, he went away.

Very soon an old beggar man came limping along on a crutch, with a countenance haggard

and miserable, and, advancing to them, held
out his cap for alms. Mr. George, who thought
it was not best to give to beggars in the streets,
was going on without regarding him ; but the

THE BEGGAR.

man hobbled on by the side of the strangers, and
seemed about to be as pertinacious as the commissioner. They went on so for a little distance,
when at length, just as the man was about giving

up in despair, Rollo put his hand in his pocket, and feeling among the money there, happened to bring up a small copper coin, which he at once and instinctively dropped into the beggar's cap. He performed the movement a little slyly, so that Mr. George did not see him. This he was able to do from the fact that the beggar was on *his* side, and not on Mr. George's, and, moreover, a little behind.

As soon as the man received the coin, he took it, put the cap on his head, and fell back out of view.

"I am glad he is gone," said Mr. George; "I was afraid he would follow us half through the town."

Rollo laughed.

"What is it?" said Mr. George. "What makes you laugh?"

"Why, the fact is," said Rollo, "I gave him a batz."

"Ah!" said Mr. George.

"Yes," said Rollo, "or something like a batz, that I had in my pocket."

A batz is a small Swiss coin, of the value of a fifth of a cent. Rollo had become familiar with this money in the course of his travels in Switzerland, but he did not yet know the names of the Prussian coins. The money which he gave the beggar was really what they called a *pfennige.**

Rollo supposed that his uncle would not quite approve of his giving the beggar this money ; but as he never liked to have any secrecy or concealment in what he did, he preferred to tell him. This is always the best way.

As soon as the beggar had gone, another commissioner came to offer his services. This time, however, Mr. George, after once telling the man that he did not wish for his services, took no further notice of him ; and so he soon went away.

The streets of Cologne are exceedingly narrow, and there are no sidewalks — or scarcely any. In one place Mr. George and Rollo passed through a street which was so narrow, that, standing in the middle and extending his hands, Mr. George could touch the buildings at the same time on each side. And yet it seemed that carriages were accustomed to pass through this street, as it was paved regularly, like the rest, and had smooth stones laid on each side of it for wheels to run in, with grooves, which seemed to have been worn in them by the wheels that had passed there.

The reason why the streets are so narrow in

* Pronounced *fenniger*

3

these old towns is, that in the ancient times, when they were laid out, there were no wheeled carriages in use, and the streets were only intended for foot passengers. When, at length, carriages came into use, the houses were all built, and so the streets could not easily be widened.

Our travellers at length reached a large, open square, on the farther side of which the immense mass of the cathedral was seen rising, like a gray and venerable ruin. The wall which formed the front of it, and which terminated above in the unfinished mason work of the towers, was very irregular in its outline on the top, having remained just as it was left when the builders stopped their work upon it, five hundred years ago. The whole front of this wall, having been formed apparently of clusters of Gothic columns, which had become darkened, and corroded, and moss-covered by time, appeared very much, as Rollo had said, like a range of cliffs — the resemblance being greatly increased by the green fringe of foliage with which the irregular outline of the top was adorned. It may seem strange that such a vegetation as this could arise and be sustained at such a vast elevation. But ancient ruins are almost always found to be thus covered with plants which grow upon them, even at a very great height above the ground, with a luxuriance

which is very surprising to those who witness this
phenomenon for the first time. The process is
this : Mosses and lichens begin to grow first on
the stones and in the mortar. The roots of these
plants strike in, and assisted by the sun and rain,
they gradually disintegrate a portion of the masonry, which, in process of time, forms a soil
sufficient for the seeds of other plants, brought by
the wind, or dropped by birds, to take root in.
At first these plants do not always come to matu-
rity ; but when they die and decay, they help to
increase the soil, and to make a better bed for
the seeds that are to come afterwards. Thus, in
the course of centuries, the upper surfaces of old
walls and towers become quite fertile in grass
and weeds, and sometimes in shrubbery. I once
gathered sprigs from quite a large rosebush
which I found growing several hundred feet
above the ground, on one of the towers of the
cathedral of Strasbourg. It was as flourishing
a rosebush as I should wish to see in any gentleman's garden.

What Rollo meant by the bears and wolves
which he said he saw looking down from these
cliff-like towers, were great stone figures of these
animals, that projected from various angles and
cornices here and there, to serve as waterspouts.

There was an immense door of entrance to the

church, at the end of a very deep, arched recess in the middle of the wall, and Mr. George and Rollo went up to it to go in. They were met at the door by another commissioner, who offered his services to show them the church. Mr. George declined this offer, and went in.

The feeling of amazement and awe which the aspect of the interior of the cathedral first awakened in the minds of our travellers was for a moment interrupted by a man in a quaint costume, who came up to them, holding a large silver salver in his hand, with money in it. He said something to Mr. George and Rollo in German. They did not understand what he said ; but his action showed that he was taking up a contribution, for something or other, from the visitors who came to see the church. Mr. George paid no attention to him, but walked on.

On looking above and around them, our travellers found themselves in the midst of a sort of forest of monstrous stone columns, which towered to a vast height above their heads, and there were lost in vaults and arches of the most stupendous magnificence and grandeur. The floor was of stone, being formed of square flags, all cracked and corroded by time. Along the sides of the church were various chapels, all adorned with great paintings, and containing altars richly furnished with silver lamps, and glittering paraphernalia of all kinds. Parties of ladies and gentlemen, strangers from all lands, were walking to and fro at leisure about the floor, looking at the paintings, or gazing up into the vaulted roofs, or studying out the inscriptions on the monuments a id sculptures which meet the eye on every hand.

All this was in the body of the church, or the *nave*, as it is called, which is in fact only the vesti- bule to the more imposing magnificence of what is beyond, in the ambulatory and in the choir. Mr. George and Rollo advanced in this direction, and at length they came to a vast screen made of a very lofty palisade of iron. They approached a door in the centre of the screen, and looking through between the iron bars, they beheld a scene of grandeur and magnificence wholly inde- scribable. The carved oak stalls, the gorgeously decorated altar, the immense candlesticks with candles twenty feet high, and the lofty ceiling with its splendid frescoes, formed a spectacle so imposing that they both gazed at it for some mo- ments in silent wonder.

" I wish we could get in,' said Rollo.

" I wish so too," said Mr. George ; " but 1 sup- pose that this is a sort of sacred place."

A moment after this, while Mr. George and Rollo were looking through this grating a sudden sound of music burst upon their ears. It was produced evidently by an organ and a choir of singers, and it seemed to come from far above their heads. The sound was at once deepened in volume by the reverberation of the vaults and arches of the cathedral, and at the same time softened in tone, so that the effect was inconceivably solemn.

"Hark!" said Mr. George.

"Where does that music come from?" said Rollo.

"Hark!" repeated Mr. George.

So Mr. George and Rollo stood still and listened almost breathlessly to the music, until it ceased.

"That was good music," said Rollo.

Mr. George made a sort of inarticulate exclamation, which seemed to imply that he had no words to express the emotion which the music awakened in his mind, and walked slowly away.

Presently they came to a place on one side, where there was a great iron gate or door in the screen, which seemed to be ajar.

"Here's a door open," said Mr. George; "let us go in here."

Rollo shrank back a little. "I'm afraid they will not let us go in here," said he. "It looks like a private place."

Rollo was always very particular, in all his

travels, to avoid every thing like intrusion. He would never go where it seemed to him doubtful whether it was proper to go. By this means he saved himself from a great many awkward predicaments that persons who act on a contrary principle often get themselves into while travelling. Mr. George was not quite so particular.

"It looks rather private," said Mr. George; "but if they do not wish us to go in, they must keep the door shut."

So he pushed the great iron gate open, and walked in. Rollo followed him, though somewhat timidly.

They passed between a row of chapels* on one side, and a high, carved partition on the other, which seemed to separate them from the choir, until, at length, they came to the end of the partition, where there was a gate that led directly into the choir. Mr. George *turned in*, followed by Rollo, and they found themselves standing in the midst of a scene of gorgeous magnificence which it is utterly impossible to describe.

---

* These chapels are recesses or alcoves along the side of the church, fitted up and furnished with altars, crucifixes, confessionals, paintings, images, and other sacred emblems connected with the ritual of the Catholic worship. They are usually raised a step or two above the floor of the church, and are separated from it by an ornamented railing, with a gate in the middle of it.

40   ROLLO ON THE RHINE.

Where the music came from.   Rollo espies a congregation.

"That is where the music came from that we heard," said Rollo, pointing upward.

Mr. George looked up where Rollo had pointed, and there he saw a gallery at a great elevation above them, with a choir of singers in front, and an enormous organ towering to a great height towards the vaulted roof behind. The choir was separated from the body of the church by ranges of columns above, and by richly-carved and ornamental screens and railings below. The ceilings were beautifully painted in fresco, and here and there were to be seen lofty windows of stained glass, antique and venerable in form, and indescribably rich and gorgeous in coloring.

After gazing about upon this scene for a few minutes with great admiration and awe, Rollo called his uncle's attention to a discovery which he suddenly made.

"See," said he; "uncle George, there is a congregation."

So saying, Rollo pointed across the choir to a sort of gateway, which was opposite to the side on which they came in, and where, through the spaces which opened between the great columns that intervened, a congregation were seen assembled. They were in a chapel which was situated in that part of the church. The chapel itself was full, and a great many persons were seated

in the various spaces rear. Mr. George and
Rollo walked across the choir, and joined this
congregation by taking a position near a pillar,
where they could see what was going on.

At a corner near a little gateway in a railing,
where the people appeared to come in, there was
a woman sitting with a brush in her hand. The
brush was wet with holy water. The people, as
they came in, — for a few came in after Rollo and
Mr. George arrived at the place, — touched their
fingers to this brush, to wet them, and then
crossed themselves with the holy water.

At the altar was a priest dressed in splendid
pontificals. He was standing with his back to
the people. There was a great number of im-
mensely tall candlesticks on each side of him, and
a great many other glittering emblems. The
priest was dressed in garments richly embroidered
with gold. There was a boy behind him dressed
also in a very singular manner. The priest and
the boy went through with a great variety of
performances before the altar, none of which
Rollo could at all understand. From time to
time the boy would ring a little bell, and the
organ and the choir of singers in the lofty gallery
would begin to play and sing ; and then, after a
short time, the music would cease, and the priest
and the boy would go on with their performances
as before.

Presently Rollo heard a sound of marching along the paved floor, and looking into the choir whence the sounds proceeded, he saw a procession formed of boys, with a priest, bearing some glittering sacred utensils of silver in his hands, at the head of them. The boys were all dressed alike. The dress consisted of a long crimson robe with a white frock over it, which came down below the waist, and a crimson cape over the frock, which covered the shoulders. Thus they were red above and below, and white in the middle.

One of these boys had a censer in his hands, and another had a little bell ; and as they came along you could see the censer swinging in the air, and the volumes of fragrant smoke rising from it, and you could hear the tinkling of the little bell. The priest advanced to the altar before which the audience were sitting, and there, while the censer was waving and the smoke was ascending, he performed various ceremonies which Rollo could not at all understand, but which seemed to interest the congregation very much, for they bowed continually, and crossed themselves, and seemed impressed with a very deep solemnity.

Presently, when the ceremony was completed, the procession returned into the choir, the priest at the head of it, just as it came.

When the procession had passed away, Mr. George made a sign for Rollo to follow him, and then walked along out through the gate where the woman was sitting with the holy water. She held out the brush to Mr. George and Rollo as they passed, but they did not take it.

" What ridiculous mummeries ! " said Rollo, in a low tone, as soon as they had got out of the hearing of the congregation.

" Yes," said Mr. George, " they seem so to us ; but I have a certain respect for all those ceremonies, since they are meant to be the worship of God."

" I thought it was the worship of images," said Rollo. " Did not you see the images ? "

" Yes," said Mr. George, " I saw them ; and perhaps we can make it out that those rites are, in reality, the worship of images ; but they are not *meant* for that. They are *meant* for 'he worship of God."

CHAPTER III.

THE GALLERIES.

"I WANT to get up upon the towers," said Rollo, "if we can."

"Yes," said Mr. George, "but I want first to go and see the tomb of the three kings."

"What is that?" asked Rollo.

"I will show you," said Mr. George. So saying, Mr. George led the way, and Rollo followed, along what is called the *ambulatory*, which is a broad space that extends all around the head of the cross in the cathedral churches of Europe, between the screen of the choir on one side and the ranges of chapels on the other. The ambulatory is usually very grand and imposing in the effect which it produces on the mind of the visitor, on account of the immense columns which border it, the loftiness of the vaulted roof, which forms a sort of sky over it above, and by the elaborate carvings and sculptures of the screen on one side, and the gorgeous decorations of the chapels on the other. Then all along the floor

there are sculptured monuments of ancient warriors armed to the teeth in marble representations
of iron and steel, while the walls are adorned
with rich paintings of immense magnitude, rep-
resenting scenes in the life of the Savior. There
seemed to Mr. George some incongruity between
the reverence evinced for the teachings and example of Jesus, in the pictures above, and the
honor paid to the barbarous valor of the fighting
old barons, in the monuments and effigies which
occupied the pavement below.

At length, at the head of the cross, exactly opposite to the centre of the high altar, which faced
the choir, in the place which seemed to be the
special place of honor, Mr. George pointed to a
small, square enclosure, or sort of projecting closet,
which was richly carved and gilded, and adorned
with a variety of ancient inscriptions.

" There," said Mr. George, " that must be the
tomb of the three kings. That is the sepulchre
which contains, as they pretend, the skulls of the
three wise men of the east, who came to Bethle-
hem to worship Jesus the night on which he was
born."

" How came they here ? " asked Rollo.

" They were at Milan about six or eight hundred years ago," said Mr. George, " and they
were plundered from the church there by a great

general, and given to the Archbishop of Cologne,
and he put them in this church. They have been
here ever since, and they are prized very highly
indeed. They are set round with gold and
precious stones, and have the names of the men
marked on them in letters formed of rubies."

"Can we see them?" asked Rollo. As he
said this he climbed up upon a little step, and attempted to look through a gilded grating in the
front of the coffer which contained the rubies.

"Yes," said Mr. George, "but we must pay the
sacristan for showing them to us. We can ask
him about them when we come down from the
galleries."

"And besides," continued Mr. George, "the
guide book says that under the floor of the church,
just in front of the tomb of the three kings, the
heart of Mary de Medicis is buried. That must
be the place."

So saying, Mr. George pointed to a large,
square flagstone, which looked somewhat different from the others around it. Rollo gazed a
moment at the stone, and then said,—

"I suppose so; but I don't care much about
these things, uncle George. Let us go up into
the towers."

"Very well," said Mr. George, "we will go
and see if we can find the way."

So our travellers went on along the ambulatory, and thence into the aisles and nave of the church, stopping, however, every few minutes to gaze at some gorgeously decorated altar, or large and beautiful painting, or quaint old effigy, or at some monument, or inscription, or antique and time-worn sculpture. There were a great many other parties of visitors, consisting of ladies and gentlemen, and sometimes children, rambling about the church at the same time. Rollo observed, as he passed these groups, that some were talking French, some German, and some English. Here and there, too, Rollo passed plain-looking people, dressed like peasants, who were kneeling before some altar or crucifix, saying their prayers or counting their beads, and wearing a very devout and solemn air. Some of these persons took no notice of Mr. George and Rollo as they passed them; but others would follow them with their eyes, scrutinizing their dress and appearance very closely until they got by, though they continued all the time to move their lips and utter inarticulate murmurings.

"I don't think those girls are attending much to their prayers," said Rollo.

"I'm afraid the girls in the Protestant churches in America do not attend to them much better," said Mr. George. "There is a great deal of

time spent in seeing how people are dressed by
worshippers in other churches than the Roman
Catholic."

At length Rollo caught a view of the man
who had held the plate for a contribution, at the
time when he and Mr. George came in at the
church door. He was walking to and fro, with
his plate in his hand, in a distant portion of the
church. Rollo immediately offered to go to him,
and ask how he and Mr. George were to get to
the towers. So he left Mr. George looking at a
great painting, and walked off in that direction.

Just before Rollo came to the man, his attention was attracted by a girl of about twelve or
thirteen years of age, who was strolling about
the church at a little distance before him, swinging her bonnet in her hand. She was very pretty,
and her dark eyes shone with a very brilliant,
but somewhat roguish expression.- She stopped
when she saw Rollo coming, and eyed him with a
mingled look of curiosity and pleasure.

Rollo, observing that this young lady appeared
not to be particularly afraid of him, thought he
would accost her.

" Do you speak French ? " said he in French,
as he was walking slowly by her. He supposed
from her appearance that she was a French girl
and so he spoke to her in that language.

The girl replied, not in French, but in English, —

" Yes, and English too."

" How did you know that I spoke English? " said Rollo, speaking now in English himself.

" By your looks," said the girl.

" What is your name? " asked Rollo.

" Tell me your name first," said the girl.

" My name is Rollo," said Rollo.

" And mine," replied the stranger, " is Minnie."

" Do you see that man out there," said Minnie, immediately after telling her name, " who is gathering the donations? Come and see what a play I will play him."

Minnie was a French girl, and so, though she had learned English, she did not speak it quite according to the established usage.

So she walked along towards the contribution man, wearing a very grave and demure expression of countenance as she went. Rollo kept by her side. As soon as they came near, the man held out his plate, hoping to receive a contribution from them. But as the plate already contained money which had been put in by former contributors, the action was precisely as if the man were offering money to the children, instead of asking it of them. So Minnie put forth her hand, and making a courtesy, took one of the

4

50   ROLLO ON THE RHINE.

Nein! nein.   How to get into the towers.

pieces of money that were in the plate, pretend-
ing to suppose that the man meant to give it to
her, and said at the same time, in French, —

"I am very much obliged to you, sir. It is
just what I wanted."

The man immediately exclaimed, " *Nein
nein!* " which is the German for No! no! and
then went on saying something in a very earnest tone, and holding out his hand for Minnie
to give him back the money. Minnie did so, and
then, looking up at Rollo with a very arch and
roguish expression of countenance, she turned
round and skipped away over the stone pavement, until she was lost from view behind an
enormous column. Rollo saw her afterwards
walking about with a gentleman and lady, the
party to which she belonged.

Rollo then asked the man who held the plate
what he should do to get up into the towers.
He asked this question in French, and the man
replied in French that he must go "to the Swiss,'
and the Swiss would give him a ticket.

" Where shall I find the Swiss? " asked Rollo

The man pointed to a distant part of the
church, where a number of people were going in
through a great iron gateway.

" You will find him there somewhere," said the
man, " and you will know him by his red dress."

Rollo reports to his uncle.

MINNIE'S ROGUERY.

So Rollo went and reported to his uncle
George, and they together went in pursuit of the

Swiss. They soon came to the great gate ; and just inside of it they saw a man dressed in a long red gown which came down to his ankles. This proved to be what they called the Swiss. On making known to him what they wanted, this man gave them a ticket, — they paying him the usual fee for it, — and then went and found a guide who was to show them up into the galleries.

The guide, taking them under his charge, led them outside the church, and then conducted them to a door leading into a small round tower, which was built at an angle of the wall. This tower, though small in size, was as high as the church, and it contained a spiral staircase of stone, which conducted up into the upper parts of the edifice. Mr. George and Rollo, however, found that they could not go up to the towers but only to what were called the galleries. But it proved in the end that they had quite enough of climbing and of walking along upon dizzy heights, in visiting these galleries, and Rollo was very willing to come down again when he had walked round the upper one of them, without ascending to the towers.

There were three of these galleries. The first was an inner one ; that is, it was inside the church. The two others were outside. The party was obliged to ascend to a vast height be-

fore they reached the first gallery. This gallery
was a very narrow passage, barely wide enough
for one person to walk in, which extended all
around the choir, with a solid wall on one side,
and arches through which they could look down
into the church below on the other. After walking along for several hundred feet, listening to
the swelling sounds of the music, which, coming
from the organ and choir below, echoed grandly
and solemnly among the vaults and arches above
them, until they reached the centre of the curve
at the head of the cross, Mr. George and Rollo
stopped, and leaned over the stone parapet, and
looked down. The parapet was very high and
very thick, and Rollo had to climb up a little
upon it before he could see over.

They gazed for a few minutes in silence, completely overwhelmed with the dizzy grandeur of
the view. It is always impossible to convey by
words any idea of the impression produced upon
the mind by looking down from any great height
upon scenes of magnificence or of beauty ; but it
would be doubly impossible in such a case as this.
Far below them in front, they could see the choir
of singers in the singing gallery, with the organ
behind them. The distance was, however, so
great that they could not distinguish the faces of
the singers, or even their persons. Then at a

vast distance, lower still, was the floor of the
choir, paved beautifully in mosaic, and with little
dots of men and women, slowly creeping, like
insects, over the surface of it. At a distance,
through the spaces between the columns, a part
of the congregation could be seen, with the
women and children at the margin of it, kneeling on the praying chairs, and a little red spot
near a gate, which Rollo thought must be the
Swiss. The whole of the interior of the choir,
which they looked down into as you would look
down into a valley from the summit of a mountain, was so magnificently decorated with paintings, mosaics, and frescoes, and enriched with
columns, monuments, sculptures, and carvings,
and there were, moreover, so many railings, and
screens, and stalls, and canopies, and altars, to
serve as furnishing for the vast interior, that the
whole view presented the appearance of a scene
of enchantment.

Mr. George said it was the most imposing
spectacle that he ever saw.

After this, the guide led our two travellers up
about a hundred feet higher still, till they came
to the first outer gallery ; and the scene which presented itself to view here would be still more difficult to describe than the other. The gallery was
very narrow, like the one within, and it led

through a perfect maze of columns, pinnacles, arches, turrets, flying buttresses, and other constructions pertaining to the exterior architecture of the church. It was like walking on a mountain in the midst of a forest of stone. The analogy was increased by the monstrous forms of bears, lions, tigers, boars, and other wild and ferocious beasts, which projected from the eaves every where to convey the water that came down from rains, out to a distance from the walls of the building. These images had deep grooves cut along their backs for the water to flow in. These grooves led to the mouths of the animals, and they were invisible to persons looking up from below, so that to observers on the ground each animal appeared perfect in his form, and was seen stretching out the whole length of his body from the cornices of the building, and pouring out the water from his mouth.

From these outer galleries Rollo could not only see the pinnacles, and turrets, and flying buttresses, of the part of the church which was finished, but he could also observe the immense works of scaffolding and machinery erected around the part which was now in progress. Men were at work hoisting up immense stones, and moving them along by a railway to the places on the walls where they were destined to go.

The yard, too, on one side, far, far down, was covered with blocks, some rough, and others already
carved and sculptured, and ready to go up. The
towers were in view too, with the monstrous
crane leaning over from the summit of one of
them ; but there seemed to be no way of getting
to them but by crossing long scaffoldings where
the masons were now at work. This Rollo
would have had no wish to do, even if the guide
had proposed to conduct him.

So, after spending half an hour in surveying
the magnificent prospect which opened every
where around them over the surrounding country, and in scrutinizing the details of the architecture near, the sculptures, the masonry, the
painted windows, the massive piers, and the buttresses hanging by magic, as it were, in the air,
and all the other wonders of the maze of archi-
tectural constructions which surrounded them, the
party began their descent.

"I am glad they are going to finish it," said
Rollo to Mr. George, as they were walking round
and round, and round and round, in the little
turret, going down the stairs. "The next time
we come here, perhaps, it will be done."

"They expect it will take twenty years to
finish it," said Mr. George.

"Twenty years ! " repeated Rollo, surprised.

"Yes," said Mr. George, "and about four millions of dollars. Why, when they first determined that they would attempt to finish it, it took fifteen years to make the repairs which were necessary in the old work, before they could begin any of the new. And now, at the rate that they are going on, it will take twenty years to finish it. For my part, I do not know whether we ought to be glad to have it finished or not, on account of the immense cost. It seems as if that money could be better expended."

"Perhaps it could," said Rollo. "But every body that comes here to see it gets a great deal of pleasure; and as an immense number of people will come, I think the amount of the pleasure will be very great in all."

"That is true," said Mr. George, "and that is the right way to consider it; but let us make the calculation in the same way that we made the calculation about the gold chain that you were going to buy in London. If we suppose that the church was half done when they left off the work, and that it will now cost four millions of dollars to finish it, that will make eight millions of dollars in all. Now, what is the interest of eight millions of dollars, say at three per cent.?"

Rollo began to calculate it in his mird; but

before he had got through, Mr. George said that it was two hundred and forty thousand dollars a year.

"That," said Mr. George, "is equal, with a proper allowance for repairs, to, say a thousand dollars per day. Now, do you think that the people who will come here to see it will get pleasure enough from it to amount in all to a thousand dollars a day?"

"I don't know," said Rollo, doubtfully. "I'd give one dollar, I know, to see it."

"Yes," said Mr. George, "so would I; and I do not know but that there would be three hundred thousand to come in a year, including all the great occasions that would bring out immense assemblages from all the surrounding country."

"At any rate, I hope they will finish it," said Rollo.

"So do I," said Mr. George.

"And I mean to put a little in the man's plate when I go down," said Rollo, "and then I shall have a share in it."

"I will too," said Mr. George.

Accordingly, as they passed by the man when they were leaving the church, Mr. George put a franc into his plate, and Rollo half a franc. Just at the time that they put their money in

One of the four millions of dollars raised.

the party that Minnie belonged to came by, and
the gentleman put in a silver coin called a thaler,
which is worth about seventy-five cents ; so that
Rollo had the satisfaction of seeing that one
of the four millions of dollars was raised on
the spot.

CHAPTER IV.

TRAVELLING ON THE RHINE.

THE steamboats and hotels, and all the arrangements made for the accommodation of travellers
on the Rhine, are entirely different from those of
any American river, partly for the reason that so
very large a portion of the travelling there is
pleasure travelling. The boats are smaller, and
they go more frequently. The company is more
select. They sit upon the deck, under the awn-
ings, all the day, looking at their guide books,
and maps, and panoramas of the river, and studying out the names and history of the villages,
and castles, and ruined towers, which they pass
on the way. The hotels are large and very elegant. They are built on the banks of the river,
or wherever there is the finest view, and the
dining room is always placed in the best part of
the house, the windows from it commanding
views of the mountains, or overlooking the water,
so that in sitting at table to eat your breakfast,
or your dinner, you have before you all the time

some charming view. Then there is usually connected with the dining room, and opening from
it, some garden or terrace, raised above the road
and the river, with seats and little tables there,
shaded by trees, or sheltered by bowers, where
ladies and gentlemen ean sit, when the weather
is pleasant, and read, or drink their tea or coffee,
or explore, with an opera glass, or a spy glass,
the scenery around. They can see the towers and
castles across the river, and follow the little paths
leading in zigzag lines up among the vineyards
to the watchtowers, and pavilions, and belvi-
deres, that are built on the pinnacles of the rocks,
or on the summits of the lower mountains.

The hotels and inns, even in the smallest villages, are very nice and elegant in all their
interior arrangements. These small villages
consist usually of a crowded collection of the
most quaint and queer-looking houses, or rather
huts, of stone, with an antique and venera-
ble-looking church in the midst of them, looking
still more quaint and queer than the houses.
The hotels, however, in these villages, or rather
on the borders of them, — for the hotels are often
built on the open ground beyond the town, where
there is room for gardens and walks, and raised
terraces aroun 1 them, — are palaces in comparison
with the dwellings of the inhabitants. And well

they may be, for the villagers are almost all laborers of a very humble class — boatmen, who get their living by plying boats up and down the river ; vinedressers, who cultivate the vineyards of the neighboring hills ; or hostlers and coach-men, who take care of the carriages and of the horses employed in the traffic of the river. A great number of horses are employed ; for not only are the carriages of such persons as choose to travel on the Rhine by land, or to make excursions on the banks of the river, drawn by them, but almost all the boats, except the steamboats that go up the river, are *towed* up by these animals. To enable them to do this, a regular tow path has been formed all the way up the river, on the left bank, and boats of all shapes and sizes are continually to be seen going up, drawn, like canal boats in America, by horses — and sometimes even by men. Once I saw some boys drawing up a small boat in this way. It seems they had been going down the stream to take a sail, or perhaps to convey a traveller down ; and now they were coming up again. drawing their boat by walking along the bank, the current being so rapid that it is much easier to draw a boat up than it is to row it. The boys had a long line attached to the mast of their boat, and both of them were drawing upon this line by means

TOWING.

Interior arrangements of the hotels.

of broad bands, forming a sort of harness, which were passed over their shoulders.

Now, the small villages that I was speaking of are formed almost exclusively of the dwellings of the various classes which I have described, while the hotels or inns that are built on the margins of them are intended, not as they would be in America, for the accommodation of the people of the same class, but for travellers of wealth, and rank, and distinction, who come from all quarters of the world to explore the beauties and study the antiquities of the Rhine. Thus the inns, however small and secluded they may be, and however retired and solitary the places in which they stand, are always very nice, and even elegant, in their interior arrangements. The chambers are furnished and arranged in the prettiest possible manner. Handsome open carriages and pretty boats are ready to convey visitors on any excursion which they may desire to make in the neighborhood, and the table is provided with almost as many delicacies and niceties as you can have in Paris.

The roads along the banks of the Rhine, too, are absolutely perfect. Well they may be so in fact, for workmen have been constantly employed in making and perfecting them for nearly two thousand years. Julius Cæsar worked upon

them. Charlemagne worked upon them. Fred-
eric the Great worked upon them. Napoleon
worked upon them. They are walled up wherever necessary on the side towards the river ; the
rock is cut away on the side towards the land ;
valleys have been filled up ; hill sides have been
terraced, and ravines bridged over ; until the
road, though passing along the margin of a very
mountainous region, is almost as level as a railway throughout the whole of its course. And as
it is macadamized throughout, and is kept in the
most perfect condition, it is always, in wet weather
as well as dry, as firm, and hard, and smooth as a
floor.

With such roads and such carriages on the
land, and such pretty steamboats as they have
upon the water, it would be very pleasant going
up through the highlands of the Rhine, if there
were nothing but the natural scenery to attract
the eye of the traveller. But besides the quaint
and ancient villages, and the curious old churches
which adorn them, — villages which sometimes
line the margin of the water, and sometimes cling
to the slopes of the hills, or nestle in the higher
valleys, — there are other still stronger attrac-
tions, in the castles, towers, and palaces, which are
seen scattered every where on the river banks,
adorning every prominent and commanding posi-

tion along the shores, and crowning, in many cases,
the summits of the hills. Many of these castles
and towers, though built originally hundreds of
years ago, are still kept in repair and inhabited,
some being used as the summer residences of
princes, or of private men of fortune, and others
being armed with cannon and garrisoned with
soldiers, are held as strongholds by the kings, or
dukes, or electors, in whose dominions they lie.
There are a great many of them, however, that
have been allowed to go to decay; and the ruins
of these still stand, presenting to the eye of the
traveller who gazes up to them from the deck of
the steamer, or from his seat in his carriage, or
who climbs up to visit them more closely, by
means of the zigzag paths which lead to them, very
interesting relics and memorials of ancient times.
The ruins are generally on very lofty summits,
and they usually occupy the most commanding
positions, so that the view from them up and
down the river is almost always very grand.
The castles were built by the dukes, and barons,
and other feudal chieftains of the middle ages,
and they are placed in these commanding positions in order that the chieftains who lived in
them might watch the river, and the roads leading along the banks of it, and come down with a
troop of their followers to exact what they called

tribute, but what those who had to pay it called plunder, from the merchants or travellers whom they saw from the windows of their watchtowers, passing up and down.

In fact these men were really robbers; being just like any other robbers, excepting that they restricted themselves to some rule and system in their plunderings, such as an enlightened regard for their own interest required. If, when they found a vessel laden with merchandise, or a company of travellers coming down the river, they had robbed them of every thing they possessed, the river and the roads would soon have been entirely abandoned, and their occupation would have been gone. In order to avoid this result, they were accustomed to content themselves with a certain portion of the value which the traveller was carrying; and they called the money which they exacted a tribute, or tax, paid for the privilege of passing through their dominions. They kept continual watch in their lofty castles, both up and down the river, to see who came by, and then, descending with a sufficient force to render resistance useless, they would take what they pretended to consider their due, and retreat with it to their almost inaccessible fastnesses, where they were safe from all pursuers.

They often had wars with one another; and in

the progress of these wars the weaker chieftains became, in the course of time, subjected to the stronger, and thus two or more small dominions would often become united into one. These amalgamations went on continually ; and as they advanced, the condition of the cultivator of the ground, and of the peaceful merchant or traveller, was improved, for the rules and regulations for the collection of the tribute became more fixed and settled, and men knew more and more what they could calculate upon, and could regulate their business accordingly. Arrangements were made, too, to collect a regular tax from the cultivators of the ground ; and just so far as these arrangements were matured, and the produce of the plunder, or the tribute, or the tax, or whatever we call it, increased, just so far it became for the interest of the chieftains that the cultivation of the land and the traffic on the river should be increased, and should be protected from all depredations but their own. Thus a system of law grew up, and arrangements for preserving public order, for promoting the general industry, and rules and regulations for the collection of the tribute, until at length, when all these arrangements were ma-tured, and the multitude of petty chieftains be-came combined under one great chieftain ruling over the whole, and collecting the revenue for his subordinates, we find a great kingdom as the result, in which the descendants of the ancient marauders that lived in castles on the hills, under the name of princes and nobles, collect the means of enabling themselves to live in idleness and luxury out of the avails of the labor of the agriculturists, the merchants, and the manufacturers, by a combined and concerted arrangement, and a regular system of rents, taxes, and tolls, instead of by irregular forrays and depredations, as in former years.

When any one of these nobles is questioned as to the nature of his claim to the enjoyment of so large a portion of the produce of the land, without doing any thing to earn or deserve it, he says that it is a *vested right ;* that is, that he has a right to claim and take a certain portion of the proceeds of the toil of the *present* generation of laborers, because his forefathers claimed and took a similar portion from theirs. And the one monarch, whose ancestors succeeded in overpowering or crowding out the others, claims his right to rule on the same ground. Thus, in the progress of ages, by a strange commutation, robbery and plunder, when systematized, and extended, and established on a permanent basis, become legitimacy, and the divine right of kings.

In America there is no such division of the

fruits of industry between those who do the work and a class of idle nobles, and soldiers, and priests who do nothing but consume the proceeds of it. There every man possesses the full fruit of his labor, except so far as he himself joins with his fellow-citizens in setting apart a portion for the purposes of public and general utility. This is the reason why such immense numbers of laboring men are every year leaving Germany and emigrating to America.

But to return to the Rhine. Of course, just so fast and so far as the smaller chieftains were conquered and dispossessed, and the country came into the hands of a smaller number of greater princes, the old castles became useless. Besides, when rules and laws, instead of surprises and violence, became the means by which contributions were levied, it was no longer necessary to have strongholds on high hills to come down from, when a vessel or a traveller was coming by, and to retreat to with the booty when the plunder had been taken. A great number of these old castles have, therefore, gone to decay; for they were generally built too high on the hills and rocks to be convenient as dwellings for peaceable men. A few of the largest and strongest of them were retained as fortresses; and those that were retained have been greatly enlarged

and strengthened in their defences in modern
times, so that some of them are now the greatest
and strongest fortresses in the world.   Others,
that were built in tolerably accessible situations,
or which commanded an unusually beautiful view,
were retained and kept in repair, and are used
now as the summer residences of wealthy men.
The rest were suffered gradually to go to decay,
and the ruins and remains of them are seen
crowning almost every remarkable height all
along the river.   Some of these ruins are still
in a very good state of preservation, so that in
going up to explore them you can make out very
easily the whole original plan of the edifice.
You can find the turret, with the remains of the
stairs which led up to the watchtower, and the
kitchen, and the hall, and the armory, and the
stables.   In others, there is nothing to be seen
but a confused mass of unintelligible ruins; and
in others still, every thing is gone, except, perhaps, some single arch or gateway, which stands
among a mass of shapeless mounds, the last remaining relic of the edifice it once adorned, and
itself tottering, perhaps, on the brink of its pre-
cipitous foundation, as if just ready to fall.

These old ruins are visited every year by thousands of persons who come from every part of
the world to see them.   These visitors arrive

DONKEY RIDING.

every year in such numbers that the steamboats, both going up and coming down, and all the hotels, and thousands of carriages, which are perpetually plying to and fro along the shores on both sides of the river, are constantly filled with them. A great many people merely pass up or down the river in a steamer, in a day and a night, and only see the ruins and the other scenery by gazing at them from the deck of the vessel. But in this case they get no idea whatever of the Rhine. It is necessary to travel slowly, to stop frequently at the towns on the bank, to make excursions along the shores and into the interior, and to ascend to the sites of the ruins, and to other elevated points, so as to view the valley and the stream meandering through it from above, or you obtain no correct idea whatever of travelling on the Rhine.

The work of ascending to the old ruins would be a very arduous and difficult one for all but the young and robust, were it not for the assistance that is afforded by the donkeys that are kept at the foot of every remarkable hill that travellers might be supposed desirous to ascend. These donkeys have a sort of chair fitted upon them, that is, a saddle, flat upon the top, and guarded all around one side by a sort of back, like the back of a chair. The trappings are covered with some kind of scarlet cloth, so that the troop of donkeys standing together under the shade of the trees, at the foot of the hill which they are to ascend, make a very gay appearance. The donkeys look very small to bear so heavy a load as a full grown person ; but they are very strong, and they carry their burden quite easily, especially as the distance is not very great. For these mountains of the Rhine, celebrated as they are for the romantic grandeur which they impart to the scenery, are, after all, seldom more than a few hundred feet high. There is also, almost always, an excellent path leading up to them. It winds usually by zigzags through the groves of trees, or between gardens and vineyards, in a very delightful manner, so that the ascent in going up any of these hills would make a very pleasant excursion even without the ruins on the top.

Such, in its general features, is the mountainous region of the Rhine, as it appears to the travellers who go to visit it at the present day ; and it was this region that Rollo and Mr. George were now going to explore.

CHAPTER V.

THE SIEBEN GEBIRGEN.

THE word *Sieben* means *seven*, and *Gebirgen* means *mountains*.* Thus the *Sieben Gebirgen* is the Seven Mountains. It is the name given to a mountainous mass of land which rises into seven or more principal peaks, just at the entrance of the romantic part of the Rhine. The highest of these mountains is the celebrated Drachenfels, which has a ruined castle on the top of it, and an inn for the accommodation of travellers just below. The Seven Mountains and Drachenfels are on the east bank of the river. Opposite to them on the left bank are some other remarkable mountains, crowned also with celebrated ruins. The river flows between these highlands as through a gateway. They form, in fact, the commencement of the mountainous region of the Rhine, in ascending the river from Cologne.†

---

* The words are pronounced as they are spelled, except that the *g* in *Gebirgen* is hard.

† The reader must be very careful to get the idea right in his

The large town next below where these mountains commence is Bonn, which is, perhaps, thirty
or forty miles above Cologne. The country up
as far as Bonn from Cologne is pretty level, and
a railroad has been made there. At Bonn the
mountains begin, and the railroad has accordingly
not been yet carried any farther. Mr. George
and Rollo went up to Bonn by the railroad.

Mr. George wished to stop at Bonn for half a
day to visit a celebrated university that is there.
The buildings of this university were formerly a
palace ; but they were afterwards given up to
the use of the university, which subsequently became one of the most distinguished seminaries of
learning in Europe. Mr. George wished to visit
this university. He had letters of introduction
to some of the professors. He wished also to
see the library and the cabinets of natural history that were there. He invited Rollo to go
with him, but Rollo concluded not to go. He
would have liked to have seen the library very
well, and the cabinets, but he was rather afraid
of the professors.

So, while Mr. George went to visit the literary
institution, Rollo amused himself by rambling

mind in respect to which way is *up* on the Rhine. The river flows
north. Of course, in looking on the map, what is *down* on the
page is *up* in respect to the flow of the river.

THE SIEBEN GEBIRGEN. 79

Rollo's ramble.   The prospect.   Going up the river.

about the town, and looking at the quaint old churches, and the houses, and the fortifications, and in strolling along the quay, by the shore of the river, to see the steamers and tow boats go up and down.

At length he went to the hotel. The hotel was just without the gates, near the river. There was a garden between the hotel and the river, with a terrace at the margin of it, over-looking the water, where there were tables and chairs ready for any person who might choose to take coffee or any other refreshments there. Mr. George's room was on this side of the hotel, and being pretty high it overlooked the gardens, and the terrace, and the river, and afforded a charming view. Up the river, on the other side, about three or four miles off, the Sieben Gebirgen were plainly to be seen, the summits of them tipped with ancient ruins.

After Rollo had been sitting there about half an hour, Mr. George came home. It was then about one o'clock.

"Well, Rollo," said he, "we are going up the river. I have engaged the landlord to send us up in a carriage to some pleasant place on the bank of the river among the mountains, where we can spend the Sabbath."

"Why, what day is it?" asked Rollo.

"It is Saturday," replied Mr. George.

Rollo was quite surprised to find that it was Saturday. In fact, in travelling on the Rhine, as there is so little to mark or distinguish one day from another, we almost always soon lose our reckoning.

"What is the name of the place where we are going?" asked Rollo.

"I don't know," replied Mr. George. "I cannot understand very well. He is going to send us somewhere. How it will turn out I cannot tell. We must trust to the fortune of war."

Mr. George often called the luck that befell him in travelling the fortune of war. "If we were contented," he would say, "to travel over and over again in places that we know, then we could make some calculations, and could know beforehand, in most cases, where we were going and how we should come out. But in travelling in new and strange places we cannot tell at all, especially when there is no language that we can communicate well with the people in. So we have to trust to the fortune of war."

Mr. George, however, determined to make one more effort to find out where he was going; and so, when the carriage came to the door, and he and Rollo were about to get into it, he asked the porter of the house — who was the man that "spoke English"—what the name of the place was where 'hey were going to stop. "Yes, sare," replied the man. "You will stop. You will go to Poppensdorf and to Kreitzberg, and then you will go to Gottesberg, and then you will go to Rolandseck, where there is a boat that will take you to Drachenfels, or to Kœnigswinter."

He said all this with so strong a German accent, and pronounced the barbarous words with so foreign an intonation, that no trace or impression whatever was left by them on Mr. George's ear.

"But which is the place," asked Mr. George, speaking very deliberately and plainly,—"which is the place where we are to be left by the carriage to stay on Sunday? Is it Rolandseck or Kœnigswinter?"

"Yes, sare," said the porter, making a very polite bow. "Yes, sare, you will go to Rolandseck, and to Kreitzberg, and to Gottesberg, and if you please you can stop at Poppensdorf."

"Very well," said Mr. George. "Tell him to drive on."

This is a tolerably fair specimen of the success to which travellers, and the porters, and waiters, who "speak English," attain to, in their attempts to understand one another. In fact, the attempts

c

of these domestic linguists to *speak* English are
sometimes still more unfortunate than their attempts to understand it. One of them, in talking to Mr. George, said "No, yes," for no, sir.
Another told Rollo that the dinner would be
ready in *fiveteen* minutes, and a very worthy
landlord, in commenting on the pleasant weather,
said that the time was very *agregable.* So a
waiter said one day that the *bifstek* was just
coming up out of the *kriken.* He meant kitchen.

The place where the porter, who engaged the
carriage for Mr. George, intended to leave him,
was really Rolandseck. Rolandseck is the name
of a ruined arch, the remains of an ancient tower
which may be seen in the engraving a little farther on, upon the height of land on the left side
of the view. The lofty ruin on the right, farther
in the distance, is Drachenfels. At the foot of
Drachenfels, a little farther down the river, —
and we are looking down the river in the engraving, — is a town called Kœnigswinter, which
is the place that people usually set out from to
ascend the mountain, a great number of donkeys
being kept there for that purpose. Beneath the
tower of Rolandseck, near the margin of the
water, is a row of three or four houses, two of
which are hotels. The land rises so suddenly
from the river here, that there is barely room for

the road and the houses between the water and the hill. In fact, the road itself is terraced up with a wall ten or fifteen feet high towards the water, and the houses in the same manner from the road. You enter them, indeed, from the level of the road ; but you are immediately obliged to ascend a staircase to reach the principal floor of the house, which is ten or fifteen feet above the road, and the gardens of the house are on terraces raised to that height by a wall. Thus from the gardens and terraces you look down fifteen feet over a wall to the road, and from the road you look down fifteen feet over a wall to the water. Along the outer margin of the road is a broad stone wall or parapet, flat at the top and about three feet high. All this you can see represented in the engraving.

In the middle of the river, opposite to the hotels, is a very beautiful island with a nunnery upon it. This island is called Nonnenwerth. Now, in regard to all these castles and churches, and other sacred edifices on the Rhine, there is almost always some old legend or romantic tale, which has come down through succeeding generations from ancient times, and which adds very much to the interest of the locality where the incidents occurred. The tale in respect to Rolandseck and Nonnenwerth is this: Roland was the nephew of the great monarch and conqueror, Charlemagne. He became engaged to the daughter of the chieftain who lived in Drachenfels, the ruins of which you see in the engraving crowning the hill on the right bank of the river, some little distance down the stream. In a battle in which he was engaged, he killed his intended father-in-law by accident, being deceived by the darkness of the night, and thinking that he was striking an enemy instead of a friend After this, he could not be married to his intended bride, the etiquette of those days forbidding that a warrior should marry one whose father he had slain. The maiden, in her grief and despair, betook herself to the nunnery on the island near her father's castle, and Roland, since he could not be permitted to visit her there, built a tower on the nearest pinnacle of the opposite shore, in order that he might live there, and at least comfort himself with a sight of the building where his beloved was confined. The story is, however, that the unhappy nun lived but a short time. Roland himself, however, continued to live in his tower, a lonely hermit, for many years.

Another version of this legend is, that the maiden was led to go to the convent and conserate herself as a nun, on account of a false report which she had heard, that Roland himself was killed i: the battle, and that when she learned that he was still alive, it was too late for her to be released from her vows. However this may be, Roland retired to this lofty tower, in order to be as near her as possible, and to be able to look down upon the dwelling where she lived. How well he could do this you can easily see by observing how finely the ruined tower on the top of the hill commands a view of the river and of the island, as well as of the nunnery itself, imbosomed in the trees.

A little below the ruin of Roland's Tower you see a pavilion on a point of the rock, which, though somewhat lower in respect to elevation, projects farther towards the stream, and consequently commands a finer view. This pavilion has been erected very lately by a gentleman who lives in one of the houses at the margin of the road, and who owns the vineyards that cover the slope of the hill. The road to it leads up among these vineyards through the gentleman's grounds, but he leaves it open in order that visitors who ascend up to Roland's Tower may go to the pavilion on the way, and enjoy the view.

It was to one of these hotels at Rolandseck that the porter at Bonn had arranged to send Mr. George, as the pleasantest place that was near to spend the Sabbath in. He could not have made a better selection.

The ride, too, in the carriage from Bonn up to Rolandseck, was delightful. Nothing could be more enchanting than the scenery which was presented to view on every hand. The carriage, like all the other private carriages used for travellers on the Rhine, was an open barouche, and when the top was down it afforded an entirely unobstructed view. The day was pleasant, and yet the sun was so obscured with clouds that it was not warm, and Rollo stood up in the carriage nearly all the way, supporting himself there by taking hold of the back of the driver's seat, and looking about him on every side, uttering continual exclamations of wonder and delight. He attempted once or twice to talk with the driver, trying him in French and English ; but the driver understood nothing but German, and so the conversation soon settled down to an occasional *Was ist das ?* from Rollo, and a long reply to the question from the driver, not a word of which Rollo was able to understand.

They passed out of Bonn by means of a most singular avenue. It was formed of a very broad space in the centre, which seemed, by its place, to have been intended for the road way ; but instead of being a road way, it was covered with a rich growth of grass, like a mowing field. On each side of this green were two rows of trees, which bordered a sort of wide sidewalk, of which there were two, one on each side of the road. These side passages were the carriage ways.

"See, uncle George," said Rollo. "The road has all grown up to grass, and we are riding on the sidewalk."

The carriage passed on, and when it reached the end of the avenue, it came to a beautiful and extensive edifice, standing in the midst of groves and gardens, which was formerly a chateau, but is now used for a museum of natural history. Here were arranged the cabinets which Mr. George had been to see that morning. Passing this place, the carriage gradually ascended a long hill, on the summit of which, half concealed by groves of trees, was an ancient-looking church. Mr. George had seen this hill before from the windows of the hotel, and knew it must be the Kreitzberg.

"He is taking us to the Kreitzberg," said Mr. George.

"What is that famous for?" asked Rollo.

"It is an ancient church, on the top of a high hill," said Mr. George, "where there is a flight of stairs made to imitate those that Jesus ascended at Jerusalem, when he went to Pilate's judgment hall. Nobody is allowed to go up or down these stairs except on their knees.

"Then, besides," continued Mr. George, looking along the page of his guide book as he spoke, "the air is so dry up at the top of this high hill, that the bodies of the old monks, who were buried there hundreds of years ago, did not corrupt, but they dried up and turned into a sort of natural mummies; and there they lie now under the church, in open coffins, in full view."

"Let us go down and see them," said Rollo

What Mr. George said was true; and these things are but a specimen of the strange and curious legends and tales that are told to the traveller, and of the extraordinary relics and wonders that are exhibited to his view, in the old churches and monasteries, which are almost as numerous as the castles, on the Rhine. The carriage, after ascending a long time, stopped at a gate by the way side, whence a long, straight road led up to the church, which stood on the very summit of the hill. Mr. George and Rollo got out and walked up. When they drew near to the church, they turned round to admire the splendor of the landscape, and to see if the carriage was still waiting for them below. They saw that the carriage still stood there, and that there was another one there too, and that a party of ladies and gentlemen were descending from it to come up and see the church. There was a little girl in this party.

"I should not wonder if that was Minnie," said Rollo.

In a short time this party, with a commissioner at the head of them, came up the walk. The girl proved to be really Minnie. She seemed very glad to see Rollo, and she stopped to speak with him while the rest of the party went on.

Rollo and Minnie followed closely behind. The commissioner led the way round to the side of the church, where there were some other ancient buildings, which were formerly a nunnery. Here they found a man who had the care of the place. He was a sacristan.* He brought a great key, and unlocked the church door, and let the party in.

The interior of the church was very quaint and queer, — as in truth the interiors of all the old churches are on the banks of the Rhine, — and was adorned with a great many curious old effigies and paintings. After waiting a few minutes for the company to look at these, the sacristan went to a place in the middle of the church

---

* A sacristan is an officer who has charge of the sacred utensils and other property of the church, and who shows them to visitors.

before the altar, and lifted up a great trap door in the floor. When the door was lifted up, a flight of steps was seen leading down under ground.

"Where are they going now?" said Minnie.

"I suppose they are going down to see the monks," said Rollo.

The party went down the stairs, Rollo and Minnie following them. The sacristan had two candles in his hands. As soon as he got to the bottom of the stairs, he passed along a narrow passage way between two rows of open coffins, placed close together side by side, and in each coffin was a dead man, his flesh dried to a mummy, his clothes all in tatters, and his face, though shrivelled and dried up, still preserving enough of the human expression to make the spectacle perfectly horrid. When Rollo and Minnie reached the place near enough to see what was there, the sacristan was moving his candles about over the coffins, one in each hand, so as to show the bodies plainly. At the first glance which Minnie obtained of this shocking sight, she uttered a scream, and ran up the stairs again as fast as she could go.

Rollo followed her, but somewhat more slowly. When he came out into the church, he caught a glimpse of Minnie's dress, as she was just making

her escape from the door. Rollo would have fol·
lowed her, but he was afraid of losing his uncle
George.

When the party, at length, came up from
their visit to the dead monks, they went to see
the sacred staircase. Rollo went with them.
The staircase seemed to be at the main entrance
to the church : the party had gone round to a
door in the side where they came in.

The sacred stairs occupied the centre of the
hall in which they were placed. There were on
the sides two plain and common flights of stairs,
for people to go up and down in the usual way.
The sacred stairs in the centre could only be
ascended and descended on the knees.

The side stairs were separated from the central flight by a solid balustrade or wall, not very
high, so that people who came to see the sacred
steps could stand on the side steps and look over.
The flight of sacred steps was very wide, and
was built of a richly variegated marble, of brown,
red, and yellow colors, intermingled together in
the stone ; and some of the stains were said
to have been produced by the blood of Christ.
Here and there, too, on the different steps of the
staircase, were to be seen little brass plates let
into the stone, beneath which were small caskets
containing sacred relics of various kinds, such as

small pieces of wood of the true cross. and fragments of the bones of saints and apostles.
Neither Mr. George nor Rollo took much interest in this exhibition ; and so, giving the sacristan a small piece of money, they went back to
their carriage. As Rollo got into the carriage
that he had come in, he saw that Minnie was
seated in hers, and she nodded her head when
Rollo's carriage moved away, to bid him good by.

Mr. George and Rollo passed one or two other
very picturesque and venerable looking ruins on
the way up the river, but they did not stop to go
and explore any of them. In one place, too,
they rode along a sort of terrace, where the
view over the river, and over the fields and vineyards beyond, was perfectly enchanting. Mr.
George said he had never before seen so beautiful a view. It was at a place where the road
had been walled up high along the side of a hill,
at some distance from the river, so that the view
from the carriage, as it moved rapidly along,
extended over the whole valley. The fields and
vineyards, the groves and orchards, the broad
river, the zigzag paths leading up the mountain
sides, the steamers and canal boats gliding up
and down over the surface of the water, and the
mountains beyond, with the rocky summit of
Drachenfels, crowned with its castle, towering

among them, combined to make the whole picture appear like a scene of enchantment.

The poet Byron described this view in three stanzas, which have been read and admired wherever the English language is spoken, and have made the name of Drachenfels more familiar to English and American ears than the name of almost any other castle on the Rhine.

DRACHENFELS.

The castled crag of Drachenfels
. Frowns o'er the wide and winding Rhine,
Whose breast of waters broadly swells
  Between the banks which bear the vine;
And hills all rich with blossomed trees,
  And fields which promise corn and wine,
And scattered cities crowning these,
  Whose far white walls along them shine,
Have strewed a scene which I should see
With double joy wert *thou* with me.

And peasant girls with deep blue eyes,
  And hands which offer early flowers,
Walk smiling o'er this paradise;
  Above, the frequent feudal towers
Through green fields lift their walls of gray;
  And many a rock which steeply lowers,
And noble arch in proud decay,
  Look o'er this vale of vintage bowers;
But one thing want these banks of Rhine —
Thy gentle hand to clasp in mine!

The river nobly foams and flows,
  The charm of this enchanted ground,
And all its thousand turns disclose
  Some fresher beauty varying round:
The haughtiest breast its wish might bound
  Through life to dwell delighted here;
Nor could on earth a spot be found
  To nature and to me so dear,
Could thy dear eyes in following mine
Still sweeten more these banks of Rhine.

In due time, Mr. George and Rollo arrived at Rolandseck, where they were received very politely by the landlord of the inn, and introduced to a very pleasant room, the windows of which commanded a fine view both of Drachenfels and of the river.

CHAPTER VI.

ROLAND'S TOWER.

" AND now," said Mr. George, as soon as the porter had put down his trunk and gone out of the room, " the first thing to be thought of is dinner."

Rollo was also ready for a dinner, especially for such excellent little dinners of beefsteaks, fried potatoes, nice bread and butter, and coffee, as his uncle usually ordered. So, after refreshing themselves a few minutes in their room, Mr. George and Rollo went down stairs in order to go into the dining room to call for a dinner. As they passed through the hall, they saw a door there which opened out upon beautifully ornamented grounds behind the house. The land ascended very suddenly, it is true, but there were broad gravel paths of easy grade to go up by ; and there were groves, and copses of shrubbery, and blooming flowers, in great abundance, on every hand. On looking up, too, Rollo saw several seats, at different elevations, where he supposed there must be good views.

While they were standing at this door, looking out upon the grounds, a waiter came by, and
they told him what they wished to have for
dinner.

"Very well," said the waiter ; "and where will
you have it ? You can have it in your room, or
in the dining room, or in the garden, just as you
please."

"Let us have it in the garden," said Rollo.

"Well," said Mr. George, "in the garden."

So the young gentlemen went out into the gar
den to choose a table and a place, while the
waiter went to make arrangements for their
dinner.

The part of the garden where the seats and
the tables were placed was a level terrace, not
behind the house, but in a line with it, at the end,
so that it fronted the road, and commanded a very
fine view both of the road and of the river, as
well as of all the people, and carriages, and
boats that were passing up and down. This terrace was high up above the road, being walled
up on that side, as I have already described ; and
there was a parapet in front, to prevent people
from falling down. This parapet was, however,
not so high but that Rollo could look over it
very conveniently, and see all that was passing
in the road and on the river below There was

a sort of roof, like an awning, over this place, to
shelter it from the sun and the rain ; and there
were trees and trellises behind, and at the ends,
to enclose it, and give it an air of seclusion.
The trellises were covered with grapevines, on
which many clusters of grapes were seen, that
had already grown quite large.   Numerous flower
pots, containing a great many brilliant flowers all
in bloom, were placed in various positions, to
enliven and adorn the scene.   Some were on the
tables, some on benches behind them, and there
were six of the finest of them placed at regular
intervals upon the parapet, on the side towards
the street.   These last gave the gardens a very
attractive appearance as seen outside, by people
going by in carriages along the road, or in boats
on the river.

Rollo and Mr. George chose a table that stood
near the parapet, in the middle of the space between two of the flower pots, and sitting down
they amused themselves by looking over the wall
until the waiter brought them their dinner.*
The dinner came at length, and the travellers
immediately, with excellent appetites, commenced
eating it.

"Uncle George," said Rollo, in the middle

* For a view of this part of the river see frontispiece.

of the dinner, "my feet are getting pretty lame."

"Are they?" said Mr. George.

"Yes," said Rollo, "I have walked a great deal lately."

"Then," said Mr. George, "you must let them rest. You must go down to the river and bathe them in the cool water after dinner, and not walk any more to-night."

"But I want to go up to Roland's Tower," said Rollo.

"Well," said Mr. George, "perhaps you might do that. You can ride up on one of the donkeys."

This plan was accordingly agreed to, and as soon as the dinner was ended it was put in execution.

The donkeys that were used for the ascent of the hill to Roland's Tower were kept standing, all caparisoned, at the foot of the hill, at the entrance to a little lane where the pathway commenced. Mr. George and Rollo had seen them standing there when they came along the road. The place was very near where they were sitting; so that, after finishing their dinner, they had only to walk a few steps through the garden, and thence out through a back gate, when they found themselves in the lane, and the donkeys and the donkey boys all before them.

Mr. George thought that he should prefer to *walk* up the mountain ; but Rollo chose a donkey, and with a little assistance from Mr. George he mounted into the seat. At first he was afraid that he might fall ; for the seat, though there was a sort of back to it, as has already been described, to keep persons in, seemed rather unsteady, especially when the donkey began to move.

"It will not do much harm if I do fall," said Rollo, " for the donkey is not much bigger than a calf."

Mr. George, who was accustomed to leave Rollo a great deal to himself on all occasions, did not stop in this instance to see him set off, but as soon as he had got him installed in his seat, began to walk himself up the pathway, with long strides, and was soon hid from view among the grapevines, at a turn of the road, leaving Rollo to his own resources with the donkey and the donkey boy. At first the donkey would not go ; but the boy soon compelled him to set out, by whipping him with the stick, and away they then went, all three together, scrambling up the steep path with a rapidity that made it quite difficult for Rollo to keep his seat.

The paths leading up these hill sides on the banks of the Rhine are entirely different from any mountain paths, or any country roads, of any sort, to be seen in America. In the first place, there is no waste land at the margin of them. Just width enough is allowed for two donkeys or mules to pass each other, and then the walls which keep up the vineyard terrace on the upper side, and enclose the vine plantings on the other, come close to the margin of it, on both sides, leaving not a foot to spare. The path is made and finished in the most perfect manner. It is gravelled hard, so that the rains may not wash it; and it mounts by regular zigzags, with seats or resting-places at the turnings, where the traveller can stop and enjoy the view. In fact, the paths are as complete and perfect as in the nature of the case it is possible for them to be made; and well they may be so, for it is perhaps fifteen hundred years since they were laid out; and during this long interval, fifty generations of vine-dressers have worked upon them to improve them and to keep them in order. In fact, it is probable that the roads and the mountain paths, both in Switzerland and on the Rhine, are more ancient than any thing else we see there, except the brooks and cascades, or the hills and mountains themselves.

When Rollo had got up about two thirds the height of the hill, he came to the pavilion, which you see in the engraving standing on a projecting

Grand view from the pavilion.

pinnacle of the rock, a little below the ruin. There was a gateway which led to the pavilion, by a sort of private path; but the gate was set open, that people might go in. Rollo dismounted from his donkey, and went in. His uncle was already there.

It is wholly impossible to describe the view which presented itself from this commanding point, both up and down the river, or to give any idea of the impression produced upon the minds of our travellers when they stood leaning over the balcony, and gazed down to the water below from the dizzy height. The pavilion is built of stone, and is secured in the most solid and substantial manner, being very far more perfect in its construction than the old towers and castles were, whose remains have stood upon these mountains so long. It will probably last, therefore, longer than they have, and perhaps to the very end of time.

It stands on a pinnacle of basaltic rock, which here projects so as actually to overhang its foundations.

The view both up and down the river is inconceivably beautiful and grand.

There was no seat in the pavilion, but there was one against the rocks, and under the shades of the trees just behind it; and here Mr. George and Rollo sat down to rest a while, after they had looked out from the pavilion itself as long as they desired.

"I believe I'll walk up the rest of the way," said Rollo, "and let the donkey stay where he is."

"Why, don't you like riding on the donkey?" asked Mr. George.

"Yes," said Rollo, "I like to ride, but he don't seem to like to carry me very well. Besides, it is not far now to the top."

The path immediately above the pavilion passed out of the region of the vineyards, and entered a little thicket of evergreen trees, through which it ascended by short zigzags, very steep, until at length it came out upon a smooth, grassy mound, which crowned the summit of the elevation; and here suddenly the ruin came into view. It was a single ruined arch, standing alone on the brink of the hill. The arch was evidently, when first built, of the plainest and rudest construction. The stones were of basalt, which is a volcanic rock, very permanent and durable in character, and as hard almost as iron. The mortar between the stones had crumbled away a good deal, but the stones themselves seemed unchanged. Mr. George struck his cane against them, and they returned a ringing sound, as if they had been made of metal.

Around this arch were the remains of the ancient wall of the building, by means of which it was easy to see that the whole edifice must have been of very small dimensions, and that it must have been originally constructed in a very rude manner. The arch seems to have been intended for a door or a window. Probably they took more pains with the construction of the arch than they did with the rest of the edifice, using larger and better stones for it, and stronger mortar; and this may be the reason why this part has stood so long, while the rest has fallen down and gone to decay. In fact, it is generally found that the arches of ancient edifices are the parts of the masonry which are the last to fall.

The opening in the arch looked down the river. Mr. George took his stand upon the line of the wall opposite the Island of Nonnenwerth, and said that he supposed there must have been another window there.

" Here is where the old knight must have stood," said he, " to look down on the island, and the convent where his lost lady was imprisoned."

" Yes," said Rollo, " he could look right down upon it from here. I wonder whether the nun knew that he was up here."

" Yes," said Mr. George, " there is not the

least doubt that she did. They found out some
way to have an understanding together, you may
depend."

After lingering about the old ruin as long as
they wished, our travellers came down the hill
again as they went up, except that Rollo
walked all the way. He was afraid to ride
on the donkey going down, for fear that he
should fall.

Rollo went down to the river side, and taking
off his stockings and shoes, bathed his feet in the
stream. While he was there a great boat came
by, towed by two horses that walked along the
bank. The rope, however, by which the horses
drew the boat was fastened, not to the side of
the boat, as is common with us on canals, but to
the top of the mast, so that it was carried high
in the air, and it passed over Rollo's head without disturbing him at all. They always have the
tow ropes fastened to the top of the mast on the
Rhine, because the banks are in some places so
high that a rope lying low would not draw.

Rollo remained on the bank of the river
some time, and then he put on his shoes and
stockings and went up into his room. He found
that his uncle George was seated at the table,
with pen, ink, and paper out, and was busy
writing letters.

"Uncle George," said Rollo, "what shall I do now?"

"Let me think," said Mr. George. Then after a moment's reflection, he added, "I should like to have you take a sheet of paper, and draw this little table up to the window, and take your seat there, and look out, and whenever you see any thing remarkable, write down what it is on the paper."

"What shall you do with it when I have got it done?" said Rollo.

"I'll tell you that when it *is* done," replied Mr. George.

"But perhaps I shall not see any thing remarkable," said Rollo.

"Then," said Mr. George, "you will not have any thing to write. You will in that case only sit and look out of the window."

"Very well," said Rollo, "I will do it. But will it do just as well for me to go down to the terrace, and do it there?"

"Yes," said Mr. George, "just as well."

So Rollo took out his portfolio and his pocket pen and inkstand, and went down to the terrace, and there he sat for nearly two hours watching what was going by, and making out his catalogue of the remarkable things. At the end of about two hours, Mr. George, having finished his letters

106   ROLLO ON THE RHINE.

Rollo's account of the remarkable things he saw from the terrace.

came down to see how Rollo was getting along.
Rollo showed him his list, and Mr. George was
quite pleased with it.   In the course of the evening
Rollo made several additions to it; and when at
length it was completed, it read as follows.

CHAPTER VII.

ROLLO'S LIST.

Remarkable Things seen from the Terrace of the Hotel at Rolandseck, by Rollo H., Saturday Even ing, August 29.

1. AN elegant steamer, painted green. Her name is the *Schiller.* She is going up the river.

2. Another steamer, the *Kœnig.* Ladies and gentlemen on the deck, under an awning.

3. I can see the ruins of Drachenfels with my spy glass, and the inn near the top of the mountain, painted white. I have been trying to find the path, to see if I could see any donkeys going up ; but I cannot find it.

4. A boat with some men and women in it putting off from the landing just above here. They are going down the stream. The current carries them down very fast. I think they are going over to the island.

No, they are going away down the river.

5. A great steamer coming *down,* with flags and banners flying.

Now she has gone by, only I can see the smoke from her smoke pipe behind the point of land.

6. The nuns are taking a walk under the trees on the island. Some of the girls of the school are going with them. The nuns are dressed in black, with bonnets partly black and partly white. The girls are dressed in pink, all alike. They are laughing and frolicking on the grass, as they go along. The nuns walk along quietly. The girls are having an excellent good time.

They are walking away down to the end of the island. The walk that they are going in is bordered by a row of poplar trees.

7. A procession of pilgrims going up to Remagen. At least, the waiter says they are pilgrims. They are in two rows, one on each side of the road, so that there is room for the carriages to pass along between them. They are dressed very queerly, like peasants. The girls and women go first, and the men come afterwards. The women have baskets, with something to eat in them, I suppose. The men have nothing. There is one man at the head, who carries a crucifix, with a wreath of flowers over it, on the top of the pole. They sing as they go along, and keep step to the music. First, the women

sing a few words, and then the men sing in response. It is a very strange sight.

8. A very swift steamer, with a great many gentlemen and ladies on board. It has gone down on the other side of the island.

9. I hear guns firing down the river.

10. A man is going by with a very long and queer-shaped wheelbarrow, and there is a dog harnessed to it before to draw, while he pushes it behind.

11. More guns firing down the river. A steamer is coming into view, with a great many flags and banners flying. The guns that I heard are on board that steamer.

The waiter says it is a company of students, from the university at Bonn, coming up on a frolic.

12. The steamer with the students is going by. There is a band of music on board, playing beautifully.

13. The steamer has stopped just above here, and all the students are going on shore.

14. The students have formed into a company on the beach, and they are marching up, with banners flying and music playing, to the terrace of a hotel, just above here.

15. The steamer has gone away up the river, and left them. There are five or six small boats

on the shore at the landing, with boatmen standing by them, waiting to be hired. I mean to ask
uncle George to let me go and take a sail in one
of them on Monday.

16. I can see the students by leaning over the
parapet and looking through my spy glass. They
are sitting at the tables under the trees on the
terrace, smoking pipes and drinking something.
They have very funny looking caps on.

17. A tow boat coming up the river. It is
drawn by two horses, that walk along the road.
The boat has a roof over it instead of a deck,
and it looks like a floating house with a family
in it.

18. A steamer coming up — the *Wilhelm*.
She came up the other side of the island.

19. A small boat going away from the landing. It is rowed by one man, with one oar,
which he works near the bow on the starboard
side. He has set the helm hard a-port, and tied
it there, and that keeps his boat from being
pulled round. I never thought of that way before.

There is a woman and a child in the stern of
the boat.

20. There is a man eating his supper on the
parapet below me, in front of the road. A girl
has brought it to him in a basket. The man

seems to be a boatman, and I think the girl is his daughter. She has a tin tea kettle with something to drink in it, and she pours it out into a mug as fast as the man wants it to drink. There is also some bread, which she breaks and gives him as fast as he wants it. There is a little child standing by, and the man stops now and then to play with her.

Now there is another man that has come and sat down by the side of him ; and a woman has brought him his supper in a basket. I think it is his wife.

21. A long raft is coming down the river. It is very long indeed. It is made of logs and boards There are twenty-two men on it, thirteen at the front end, and nine at the back end. They have got two monstrous great oars out ; one of these oars runs out at the front end of the raft, and the other at the back end, and the men are rowing. There are six men taking hold of each of these oars and working them, trying to row the raft more into the middle of the river.

There is a small house on the middle of the raft, and a fire in a large flat box near the door of it. I should think it would set the raft on fire. This fire is for cooking, I suppose, for there is a kettle hanging over it.

22. Now the students are singing a song.

23. There is a great fleet of large boats

112   ROLLO ON THE RHINE.

The steamer and the fleet of boats.   The tipsy student.

coming up the river, with a steamboat at the head of them. They come very slowly.

24. The students have finished their drinking and smoking, and are beginning to come out into the road. They are walking about there and frolicking.

25. The great fleet of boats have come up so that I can see them. They are great canal boats, towed by a steamer. There are seven of them in all. The steamer has hard work to get them along against the current. It is just as much as she can do.

26. Four of the students are getting into a small boat. One of them has a flag. Now they are putting off from the shore. They are going out to take a sail. .

27. The fleet of boats is now just opposite to the window.

28. A large open carriage, with a family in it, is riding by. There is a trunk on behind ; so I suppose they are travellers, going to see the Rhine.

29. Three of the students are walking by here. One of them — the middle one — is so tipsy that he cannot walk straight, and the others are taking hold of his arms and holding him up. I suppose they are going to see if they cannot walk him sober.

They have gone off away down the road.

30. Here comes an elegant carriage and two outriders. The outriders are dressed in a sort of uniform, and they are riding on horseback a little way before the carriage. They go very fast. There is a gentleman and a lady in the carriage.

Now they have gone by.

31. Several parties of students have gone by, to take a walk down the road. Some of them are walking along very steadily, but there are several that look pretty tipsy.

Here are three or four of them coming back, riding the donkeys. They are singing and laughing, and making a great deal of fun.

32. Here is a family of poor peasants coming down the river. They look very poor. The woman has a very queer cap on. She has one child strapped across her back, and she is leading another. There is a man and a large boy. They have packs on their backs. I wonder if they are not emigrants going to America.

33. One of the students has got hurt. I can see him down the road limping. There are two other students with him, helping him.

They are going to bring him home. They have taken a cane, and are holding it across between them, and he is sitting on it and putting his arms about their necks. Each student holds

8

one end of the cane, and so they are bringing him along.

THE STUDENTS.

The cane has broken, and let the lame student fall down.

They have got another cane, stronger, and now they are carrying him again.

The tow boat drawn by a woman.   The embarkation of the students.

Now they are stopping to rest right opposite to this hou.~e. They have changed hands, and are now carrying him again.

34. Here is a woman coming along up the river drawing a small boat. She has a band over her shoulders, and a long line attached to it, and the other end of the line is fastened to the mast of the small boat. There is a man in the boat steering. I think the man ought to come to the shore and draw, and let the woman stay in the boat and steer, for it seems very hard work to pull the boat along.

35. A boat with two women in it, and a man to row, is going across the river to the Nuns' Island. Now they are landing. The women are walking up towards the nunnery, under the trees, and the man is fastening his boat.

36. The students are gathering on the land-ing. I think that, perhaps, they are going back to Bonn in small boats. It is beginning to be dark, and time for them to go home.* Yes, they are crowding into two or three boats. The boats are getting very full. If they are not care-ful they will upset.

The boats are pushing off from the shore.

* This Rollo wrote in the latter part of the evening, in his room.

There are three boats, with two flags flying in each. They are drifting out into the current. The students have got one or two oars out, but they are not rowing much. The current carries them down fast enough without rowing.

37. I can hear the bells ringing or tolling, away down the river, the air is so still. I think it must be the bells of Bonn.

38. The students' boats are all drifting down just opposite our windows. They are going side-wise, and backwards, and every way, and are all entangled together. The students on board are calling out to one another, and laughing, and having a great time. Some of them are trying to sing, but the rest will not listen. If they are not very careful they will upset some of those boats before they get to Bonn.

39. Here comes a carriage driving slowly down the road, with four students in it. Two of them are hanging down their heads and holding them with their hands, as if they had dreadful headaches. They look very sick. The other two students seem pretty well. I suppose they are going in the carriage with the sick ones to take care of them.

It is getting too dark for me to see any more

CHAPTER VIII.

A SABBATH ON THE RHINE.

ABOUT eight o'clock the next morning, Mr.
George and Rollo went up among the gardens
behind the hotel, and after ascending for some
time, they came at length to a seat in a bower
which commanded a very fine view, and here they
sat down.

Mr. George took a small Bible out of his
pocket, and opened it at the book of the Acts,
and began to read. He continued to read for
half an hour or more, and to explain to Rollo
what he read about. Rollo was very much interested in the stories of what the apostles did in
their first efforts for planting Christianity, and of
the toils and dangers which they encountered,
and the sufferings which they endured.

At length, after finishing the reading, Mr.
George proposed that they should go down to
breakfast.

So they went down the winding walks again
which led to the inn. There they found, on the

118 ROLLO ON THE RHINE.

The order for breakfast.   The German talking English.

front side of the house, a very pleasant dining room, with tables set in it, some large and some small. Mr. George and Rollo took their seats at a small front table near a window, where they could look out over the water. Here a waiter came to them, and they told him what they would have for breakfast.

"I will have a beefsteak," said Mr. George, "and my nephew will have an omelet. We should like some fried potatoes too, and some coffee."

"*Ja,** monsieur," said the waiter. "Let us see. You will have one bifstek, one omelet, two fried potatoes, and two caffys."

"Yes," said Mr. George.

"Varry well," said the waiter. "It shall be ready in fivetoen minutes."

So the waiter went away.

"We shall want more than two fried potatoes," said Rollo, looking very serious.

"O, he means two portions," replied Mr. George; "that is to say, enough for two people. He will bring us plenty, you may depend."

Rollo and Mr. George sat by the window in the dining room until the breakfast was brought in. Besides the things which they had called for,

* Pronounced *va*ᵗ.

the waiter brought them some rolls of very nice
and tender bread, and some delicious butter. He
also brought a large plate full of fried potatoes,
and the beefsteak which came for Mr. George
was very juicy and rich. The omelet which
Rollo had chosen for his principal dish was excellent too. He made an exchange with Mr.
George, giving him a piece of his omelet, and
taking a part of the steak. Thus they ate their
breakfast very happily together, looking out the
window from time to time to see the steamboats
and the carriages go by, and to view the magnificent scenery of the opposite shores.

"I'll tell you what it is, Rollo," said Mr.
George ; "people may say what they please about
the castles and the ruins on the Rhine — I think
that the inns and breakfasts on the Rhine are
by no means to be despised."

"I think so too," said Rollo.

When they had nearly finished their breakfast,
Mr. George asked the waiter what churches there
were in the neighborhood. The waiter said there
was a church on the Island of Nonnenwerth, be-
longing to the convent, and that there was another
up the river a few miles, at the village of Remagen.

"We might go over to the island this morning,
and up to Remagen this afternoon," said Mr.
George, "only you are too lame to walk so far.'

"No, sir," said Rollo, decidedly; "my feet are well to-day. I can walk as well as not."

A few minutes after this, the waiter came to tell Mr. George that the master of the hotel was himself going over to the convent to attend church, and that he and Rollo could go in the same boat if they pleased. The boat would go at about a quarter before ten.

Mr. George said that he should like this arrangement very much; and accordingly, at the appointed time, he and Rollo set out from the inn in company with the landlord. They walked along the road a short distance, and then went down a flight of steps that led to the landing. Here there was a number of boats drawn up upon the beach. One of them had a boatman in attendance upon it, waiting for the company that he was to take over to the island.

Besides the landlord and his two guests, there were two or three girls waiting on the beach, who seemed to be going over too. All these people got into the boat, and then the boatman, after embarking himself, pushed it off from the shore.

It was a very pleasant summer morning, and Rollo had a delightful sail in going over to the island. Mr. George and the landlord talked together nearly all the way; but Rollo did not

Sailing over to the island.   Landing

listen much to their conversation, as he could not
understand the landlord very well, notwithstanding that the language which he used was English. He was seated next to the girls ; but he did
not speak to them, as he felt sure that they did
not know any language but German. So he
amused himself with looking at the hills on the
shore, and at the gardens and vineyards which
adorned them, and in tracing out the zigzag paths
which led up to the arbors and summer houses,
and to the ancient ruins. He attempted at one
time to look down into the water by the side
of the boat, to see if he could see any fishes ;
but the water of the Rhine is very turbid, and
he could not see down into it at all.

At length the boat came to the land in a little
cove on the side of the island, where there was a
sandy beach, under the shade of some ancient
trees. There was a path leading from this place
up towards the convent. The party in the boat
landed, and began to walk up this path. Mr.
George and the landlord were first, and Rollo
came next.

The little path that they were walking in came
out into another which led along among the
fields that extended down the island. There was
a nun coming up this path, leading one of the
schoolgirls. It seems they had been to take a

walk. The nun had her face shaded by a large cap, or bonnet, with a veil over it; and though

THE NUN.

she looked pale, her countenance had a very gentle expression, and was very beautiful. She bowed to the party that was coming up from the boat, and went on before them to the church.

"I wonder whether she is happy," thought Rollo to himself, "in living on this island, a nun. I wish I knew where her father and mother live, and how she came to be here, such a beautiful young lady."

This nun was indeed very beautiful, though she was an exception to the general rule, for nuns are often very plain.

The church formed a part of the convent building. It was, in fact, only a small chapel, built in a wing of the convent, with a little cupola and a bell over it. The bell was ringing when the party from the boat went up towards the edifice. On entering Rollo found that the room was very small. At the upper end was a platform, with an altar and a crucifix at the farther end of it. The altar had very tall candles upon it, and several bouquets of flowers. The candles were lighted.

Below the platform, in the place where the congregation would usually be, there were two rows of seats, like pews, with small benches before each seat to kneel upon, and also a support to lean upon in time of prayer. These seats were very few, and there were but few people sitting on them. The people that were there seemed to be the servants of the convent. Mr. George and Rollo, and the people that came with them, were the only strangers. Rollo looked around for the nuns and for the girls of the school, but they were nowhere to be seen.

As soon as Rollo had taken his seat, he observed that, though there was no minister or priest at the altar, the service was going on. He could hear a female voice, which appeared to issue from some place in a gallery behind him, out of view, reading what seemed to be verses from the Bible, in a very sweet and plaintive tone, and at the close of each verse all the people in the congregation below would say something in a responding voice together.

" Do you suppose that that is one of the nuns ? " whispered Rollo to his uncle.

" Yes," said Mr. George, " probably it is."

" This is a Catholic church, is it not ? " asked Rollo.

" Yes," said Mr. George, " almost all the churches on the Rhine are Catholic churches ; and nunneries are _always_ Catholic."

Rollo said no more, but attended to the service.

There was nothing that was said or done that Rollo could at all understand ; and yet the scene itself was invested with a certain solemnity

which produced a strong and quite salutary impression on his mind. By and by a priest, dressed
in his pontifical robes, came in by a side door,
and taking his place before the altar, with an
attendant kneeling behind him, or by his side,
went through a great number of ceremonies, of
which Rollo understood nothing from beginning to end. Mr. George, however, explained
the general nature of the performance to him that
afternoon when they were walking up the river
to Remagen, in a conversation which I shall relate in due time.

The service was concluded in about an hour,
and then the congregation was dismissed. All
but the party that came in the boat went out by
a side door which led into the other apartments
of the convent. The boat party went down to
the shore, and getting into the boat were rowed
back across the water.

After dinner, Mr. George and Rollo set out to
walk up the river to Remagen, in order to attend
church there. It was during this walk that they
had the conversation I have referred to on the
subject of the service which they had witnessed
in the little chapel at the nunnery.

"You must understand," said Mr. George,
" that the nature and design of the ceremonies of
public worship in a Protestant and in a Catholic

church are essentially and totally distinct. The Protestants meet to offer up their common prayers and supplications to God, and to listen to the instructions which the minister gives them in respect to their duties. The Catholics, on the other hand, meet to have a sacrifice performed, as an atonement for their sins. The Protestants think that all the atonement which is necessary for the sins of the whole world has already been made by the sufferings and death of Christ. The Catholics think that a new sacrifice must be made for them from time to time by the priest; and they come together to kneel before the altar while he makes it, in order that they may have a share in the benefits of it. Thus the Protestant comes to church to hear something said; the Catholic to witness something done. This is one reason, in fact, why the Catholic churches may very properly be enormously large. The people who assemble in them do not come to hear, so much as to see, or rather to be present and know what is going on, and to take part in it in heart.

"The great thing that is done," continued Mr. George, "is the receiving of the communion, that is. of the bread and wine of the Lord's supper, which they suppose is renewing the sacrifice of Christ, for the benefit of those who are presen' at the ceremony. Did you see the man who was kneeling at the foot of the steps of the altar while the priest was performing, and who brought two little silver vessels, out of which he poured something into the priest's cup?"

"Yes," said Rollo. "The silver vessels were on a little shelf at first, at the side of the altar, and he went at the proper time and kneeled with them by the side of the priest, until the priest was ready to take them."

"One of these vessels," continued Mr. George, "contained wine, the other water. When the priest held his large silver cup out to him, the man poured some of the wine into it."

"Yes," said Rollo. "And I saw the priest wiping out the cup very carefully, with a large white napkin, before he held it out for the wine."

"True," said Mr. George. "When he took the wine in his cup, it was common wine, in its natural state; but afterwards, by being conse-crated to the service of the mass, it was changed, they all believe, into the blood of Christ. It looked, they knew, just as it did before; but though it thus still retained all the appearance of wine, they believe that it became really and truly the blood of Christ, and that the priest in drinking it would make a sacrifice of Christ anew for the salvation of the souls of those who should witness and join in the ceremony.

" In the same manner a small round piece of bread, shaped like a large wafer, when consecrated by the priest's prayers, becomes, they think, really and truly the body of Christ; and the priest by eating it performs a sacrifice, just as he does by drinking the wine. When he has consecrated this wafer, he holds it up for a moment, that the people may look upon it; and they, in looking upon it, think they see a portion of the true body of Christ, which is about to be offered up by the priest as a sacrifice for their sins."

" Yes," said Rollo, " I remember when he held up the wafer. I did not know what it was."

" Did you not see that all the people bowed their heads just then," rejoined Mr. George, " and said something to themselves in a very reverent manner."

" Yes," said Rollo, " but I did not understand what it meant."

" Thus you see," continued Mr. George, " that the essential thing at a Catholic service like this, as they regard it, is the eating of the body and the drinking of the blood of Jesus Christ, as a new sacrifice for the sins of the people who are present and consenting in heart to the ceremony.

The subordinate ceremonies.

There are a great many subordinate operations and rites. The assistant goes back and forth a great many times from one side of the altar to the other, stopping to bow and kneel every time he passes the crucifix. The priest makes a great deal of ceremony of wiping out the cup before he receives the wine. Then there is a long service, which he reads in a low voice, and there are many prayers which he offers, and he turns to various passages of the Scriptures, and reads portions here and there. The people do not hear any thing that he says and does, nor is it necessary, according to their ideas of the service, that they should do so ; for they know very well that the priest is consecrating the bread or the wine, and changing it into the body and the blood of Christ, in order that it may be ready for the sacrifice. Then, when the wine is changed, the priest drinks it in a very solemn manner, raising it to his lips three several times, so as to take it in three portions. Then he holds the cup out to his assistant again, who pours a little water into it from his other vessel ; and the priest then, after moving the cup round and round, to be sure that the water mixes itself well with the wine which was left on the inner service of the cup, drinks that too. He does this in order to make sure that no portion of the precious blood remains in

9

the cup.   He then wipes it out carefully with his napkin, and puts it away."

"Yes," said Rollo, "I saw all those things. And after he had got through, he covered the cup with a cloth, embroidered with gold, and carried it away."

"And after that," continued Rollo, "the assistant, with an extinguisher on the top of a tall pole, put out the candles, and then *he* went away."

"Yes," said Mr. George, and so the service was concluded.

"Thus you see," continued Mr. George, "that for all that the people come for, to such a service as that, it was not necessary that they should hear at all. There was not any thing to be *said* *to* them. There was only something to be *done* *for* them; and so long as it was done, and done properly, they standing by and consenting, it was not of much consequence whether they could see and hear or not. So the priest turned his face away from them towards the altar; and when he had any thing to say, he spoke the words in a very low and inaudible voice."

"It is impossible," said Rollo, after a short pause, "that the wine should become blood, and the wafer flesh, while they yet look just as they did before."

THE EMIGRANTS

" True," said Mr. George, " it seems impossible to us, who hear of it for the first time, after we have grown up to years of discretion; but that does not prevent its being honestly believed by people that have been taught to consider it true from their earliest infancy."

" Do you suppose the priests themselves believe it ? " asked Rollo.

" Yes," said Mr. George, " a great many of them undoubtedly do. We find, it is true, every where, that the most intelligent and well educated men will continue, all their lives, to believe very strange things, provided they were taught to believe them when they were very young ; and provided, also, that their worldly interests are in any way concerned in their continuing to believe them."

Just at this time, Rollo's attention was attracted to what seemed to be an encampment on the roadside at a little distance before them. It was a family of emigrants that were going down the river, and had stopped to rest. The horses had been unharnessed, and were eating, and the wagon was surrounded with a family consisting of men, women, and children, who were sitting on the bank taking their suppers. Rollo wished very much that he understood German, so as to go and talk with them. But he did not, and so he contented himself with wishing them *guten abend,* which means good evening, as he went by.

He went on after this, without any farther adventure, to the village, and after attending church there, he returned with his uncle down along the bank of the river to the hotel.

Some of the old castles on the Rhine are kept in repair.

CHAPTER IX.

EHRENBREITSTEIN.

THE people of the Rhine have not allowed all the old castles to go to ruin. Some have been carefully preserved from age to age, and never allowed to go out of repair. Others that had gone to decay, or had been destroyed in the wars, have been repaired and rebuilt in modern times, and are now in better condition thar ever.

Some of the strongholds that have thus been restored are now great fortresses, held by the governors of the states and kingdoms that border on the river ; others of them are fitted up as summer residences for the persons, whether princes or private people, that happen to own them. About midway between the beginning and the end of the mountainous region of the Rhine is a place where there are two very important works of this kind. One of them is far the largest and most important of all on the river. This is the Castle of Ehrenbreitstein. Ehrenbreitstein is not only a very strong and important fortification, but it guards a very important point.

This point is the place where the River Moselle, one of the principal branches of the Rhine, comes in. The valley of the Moselle is a very rich and fertile one, and in proportion to its extent is almost as valuable as that of the Rhine. The junction of the two rivers is the place for defending both of these valleys, and has consequently, in all ages of the world, been a very important post. The Romans built a town here, in the days of Julius Cæsar, and the town has continued to the present day. It is called Coblenz. The Romans named it originally *Confluentes*, which means the *confluence ;* and this name, in the course of ages, has gradually become changed to Coblenz.

Coblenz is built on a three-cornered piece of flat land, exactly on the point where the two rivers come together. There is a bridge over the mouth of the Moselle where it comes into the Rhine, and another over the Rhine itself. The bridge over the Moselle is of stone, and was built a great many hundred years ago. That over the Rhine is what is called a bridge of boats.

A row of large and solid boats is anchored in the river, side by side, with their heads up the stream, and then the bridge is made by a plat-

The bridge of boats across the Rhine.

form which extends across from boat to boat, across the whole breadth of the stream.

Near the Coblenz side of the bridge there are two or three lengths of it which can be taken out when necessary, in order to let the steamers, or rafts, or tow boats, that may be coming up or down the river, pass through. Rollo was very much interested, while he remained at Coblenz, in looking out from the windows of his hotel, which faced the river, and seeing them open this bridge, to let the steamers and vessels pass through. A length of the bridge, consisting sometimes of *two* boats with the platform over it, and sometimes of *three*, would separate from the others, and float down the stream until it cleared itself from the rest of the bridge, and then would move by some mysterious means to one side, and so make an opening. Then, when the steamer, or whatever else it was, had passed through, the detached portion of the bridge would come back again slowly and carefully to its place.

Of course all the travel on the bridge would be interrupted during this operation ; but as soon as the connection was again restored, the streams of people would immediately begin to move again over the bridge, as before.

Across the bridge, on the heights upon the other side, Rollo could see the great Castle of

Ehrenbreitstein, together with an innumerable multitude of walls, parapets, bastions, towers, battlements, and other constructions pertaining to such a work.

One day Mr. George and Rollo went over to see this fortress. They were stopped a few minutes at the bridge, by a steamer going through. There was a large company of soldiers stopped too, part of the garrison of Ehrenbreitstein that had been over to attend a parade on the public square at Coblenz, and were now going home, so that Rollo was not sorry for the detention, as it gave him a fine opportunity to see the soldiers, and to examine the Prussian uniform. It consisted of a blue frock coat and white trousers, with an elegant brass-mounted helmet for a cap.

The way up to the castle was by a long and winding road, built up artificially on arches of solid masonry. This road was every where overlooked by walls, with portholes and embrasures for cannon, and all along it, at short distances, were immense gateways exceedingly massive and strong, which could all be shut in time of siege. When Mr. George and Rollo reached the top of the castle, they found a great esplanade there, surrounded with buildings for barracks, and for the storing of arms and provisions. The view

from this esplanade was magnificent beyond description. You could see far up and down the
River Rhine, and far *up* the Moselle, while all
Coblenz, and the two bridges, and the town below the castle, and three other immense forts that
stood on the other side of the river, were directly
beneath.

Rollo went into some of the barracks, and also
up to the top of the buildings. The buildings
were all arched over above, and covered with
earth ten feet deep, with grass growing on the
top. The men were mowing this grass when
Mr. George and Rollo were there. The object
of this earth on the roofs of the buildings is to
prevent the bombshells of the enemy from break-
ing down through the roofs and killing the men.

On the afternoon of the same day that Mr.
George and Rollo visited Ehrenbreitstein, they
went up the river a few miles in a boat to see a
smaller castle, which has been repaired and
changed into a private residence. The name of
it is Stoltzenfels. They rode up the mountain
that this castle was built upon on donkeys.
The road was very good, but the place was so
steep that it was necessary to make it twist and
turn, in winding its way up, in the most extraordinary manner. In one place it actually went
over itself by an arched bridge thrown across

the ravine. In fact, this path was just like a corkscrew.

Rollo was exceedingly delighted with the cas-tle of Stoltzenfels. A man who was there con-ducted him and his uncle, together with a small company of other visitors who arrived at the same time, all over it. It would be impossible to describe it, there were so many curious courts, and towers, and winding passage ways, and little gardens, and terraces, all built in a sort of nest among the rocks, of the most irregular and wildest character.

The rooms were all beautifully finished and furnished, and they were full of old relics of feudal times. The floors were of polished oak and the visitors, when walking over them, wore over their boots and shoes great slippers made of felt, which were provided there for the purpose

ROLLO'S LETTER. 141

Rollo writes a letter to his cousin Jenny. St. Goar.

CHAPTER X.

ROLLO'S LETTER.

AT one place where Mr. George and Rollo stopped to spend a night, Rollo wrote a letter to Jenny. It was as follows : —

ST. GOAR ON THE RHINE.
Friday Evening.

DEAR JENNY: We have got into a very lonely place. I did not know there was such a lonely place on the Rhine. The name of it is St. Goar ; but they pronounce it St. *Gwar.* The river is shut in closely by the mountains on both sides, and also above and below ; so that it seems as if we were in a very deep valley, with a pond of water in the bottom of it.

Away across the river is a long row of white houses, crowded in between the edge of the water and the mountain. On the mountain above is an old ruined castle, called the Cat. There is another old ruin a few miles below, called the Mouse. I can see both of these ruins from my windows.

There is a little town on this side of the vil·
lage too. We went out this morning to see it.
It is very small, and the streets are very narrow.
We came to the queerest old church you ever
saw. It was all entangled up with other build·
ings, and there were so many arches, and flights
of steps, and various courts all around it, that it
was a long time before we could find out where
the door was.

While we were looking about, a little girl
came up and asked us something. We supposed
she asked us whether we wished to see the church ;
so we said *Ja*, and then she ran away. Presently
we saw a boy coming along, and *he* asked us
something, and we said *Ja ;* and then he ran away.
We did not know what they meant by going
away ; but the fact was, they went to find some
men who kept the keys. It seems there are two
men who keep keys, and the girl went for one
and the boy for the other ; and so, after we
had waited about five minutes under an arch
which led to an old door, *two* men came with
keys to let us in. Uncle George paid them both,
because he said the second man that came looked
disappointed. He paid the girl and the boy
too ; so he had four persons to pay ; and when
we got in, we found that it was nothing but a
Protestant church, after all. I like the Catholic

ROLLO'S LETTER. 143

Rollo's description of the Catholic church.   The ruin of Rheinfels.

churches the best. They are a great deal the funniest.

We went to see the Catholic church afterwards. There was a monstrous old gallery all on one side of the church, and none on the other. Then there was an organ away up in a loft, and all sorts of old images and statues. I never saw such an old looking place.

As we walked along the streets, or rather the pathways between the houses, we could see the rocks and mountains away up over our heads, almost hanging over the town. They are very pretty rocks, being all green, with grapevines and bushes.

Close by the town too, up a long and very steep path, is a monstrous old ruin. The name of it is Rheinfels. I can see it from the balcony of my windows. Besides, uncle George and I went up to it this afternoon. It is nothing but old walls, and arches, and dark dungeons, all tumbling down. There was a little fence and a gate across the entrance, and the gate was locked. But there was a man who asked us something in German ; but we could see it all just as well without going in ; so we said *Nein*, which means no.

They say that a great many years ago the French took this castle, and then, to prevent its doing the enemy any good forever afterwards,

they put a great deal of gunpowder into the
cellars, and blew it up. I did not care much
about the old ruins, but I should have liked very
well to have seen them blow it up.

The waiter has just come to call us to go out
and hear the echo, and so I must go. I will tell
you about it afterwards.

The man played on a trumpet down on the
bank of the river, and we could hear the echo
from the rocks and mountains on the other side.
He also fired a gun two or three times. After
the gun was fired, for a few minutes all was still;
but then there came back a sharp crack from the
other shore, and then a long, rumbling sound from
up the river and down the river, like a peal of
distant thunder.

It is a gloomy place here after all, and I shall
be glad when I get out of it; for the river is
down in the bottom of such a deep gorge, that we
cannot see out any where. There are some old
castles about on the hills, and they look pretty
enough at a distance; but when you get near them
they are nothing but old walls all tumbling down.
The vineyards are not pretty either. They are
all on terraces kept up by long stone walls; and
when you are down on the river, and look up to
them, you cannot see any thing but the walls,
with the edge of the vineyards, like a little green

How the vineyards on the Rhine look.

fringe, along on the top. But there is no great loss in this for the vineyards are not pretty when you can see them. They look just like fields full of beans growing on short poles.

I shall be glad when we get out of this place; but uncle George says he is going to stay here all day to-morrow, to write letters and to bring up his journal. But never mind ; I can have a pretty good time sitting on the steps that go down to the water, and seeing the vessels, and steamboats, and rafts go by.

Your affectionate cousin,

ROLLO.

P. S. The Cat and the Mouse used to fight each other in old times, and the Mouse used to beat   Was not that funny?

10

CHAPTER XI.

THE RAFT.

THE morning after Rollo had finished the letter to Jenny, as recorded in the last chapter, his uncle George told him at breakfast time that he might amuse himself that day in any way he pleased.

"I shall be busy writing," said Mr. George, "nearly all the morning. It is such a still and quiet place here that I think I had better stay and finish up my writing. Besides, it must be an economical place, I think, and we can stay here a day cheaper than we can farther up the river, at the large towns."

"Shall we come to the large towns soon?" asked Rollo.

"Yes," replied his uncle. "This deep gorge only continues fifteen or twenty miles farther, and then we come out into open country, and to the region of large towns. You see there is no occasion for any other towns in this part of the Rhine than villages of vinedressers, except here and there a little city where a branch river comes in."

" Well," said Rollo, " I shall be glad when we get out. But I will go down to the shore, and play about there for a while."

Accordingly, as soon as Rollo had finished his breakfast, he went down to the shore.

The hotel faced the river, though there was a road outside of it, between it and the water. From the outer edge of the road there was a steep slope, leading down to the water's edge. This slope was paved with stones, to prevent the earth from being washed away by the water in times of flood. Here and there along this slope were steps leading down to the water. At the foot of these steps were boats, and opposite to them, in the road, there were boatmen stand- ing in groups here and there, ready to take any body across the river that wished to go.

Rollo went down to the shore, and took his seat on the upper step of one of the stairways, and began to look about him over the water. There were two other boys sitting near by ; but Rollo could not talk to them, for they knew only German.

Presently one of the boatmen came up to him, and pointing to a boat, asked him a question. Rollo did not understand what the man said, but he supposed that he was asking him if he did not wish for a boat. So Rollo said *Nein*, and the man went away.

There was a village across the river, in full view from where Rollo sat. This village consisted of a row of white stone houses facing the river, and extending along the margin of it, at the foot of the mountains. There seemed to be just room for them between the mountains and the shore. Among the houses was to be seen, here and there, the spire of an antique church, or an old tower, or a ruined wall. After sitting quietly on the steps until he had seen two steamers go down, and a fleet of canal boats from Holland towed up, Rollo took it into his head that it might be a good plan for him to go across the river. So he went in to ask his uncle George if he thought it would be safe for him to go.

"You will take a boatman?" said Mr. George.

"Yes," said Rollo.

"And how long shall you wish to be gone?"

"About an hour," said Rollo.

"Very well," said Mr. George, "you may go."

So Rollo went down to the shore again, and as he now began to look at the boats as if he wished to get into one of them, a man came to him again, and asked him the same question. Rollo said *Ja*. So the man went down to his boat, and drew it up to the lowest step of the stairs where Rollo was standing. Rollo got in, and taking his seat, pointed over to the other side of the river. The man then pushed off. The current was, however, very swift, and so the boatman poled the boat far up the stream before he would venture to put out into it; and then he was carried down a great way in going across.

When they reached the landing on the opposite shore, Rollo asked the man, " How much ? " He knew what the German was for how much. The man said, " Two groschen." So Rollo took the two groschen from his pocket and paid him. Two groschen are about five cents.

Rollo walked about in the village where he had landed for nearly half an hour; and then, taking another boat on that side, he returned as he had come. On his way back he saw a great raft coming down. He immediately conceived the idea of taking a little sail on that raft, down the river. He wanted to see "how it would seem" to be on such an immense raft, and how the men managed it. So he went in to propose the plan to his uncle George. He said that he should like to go down the river a little way on the raft, and then walk back.

" Yes," said Mr. George, " or you might come up in the next steamer."

"So I might," said Rollo.

"I have no objection," said Mr. George.

"How far down may I go?" said Rollo.

"Why, you had better not go more than ten or fifteen miles," said Mr. George, "for the raft goes slowly, — probably not more than two or three miles an hour, — and it would take you four or five hours, perhaps, to go down ten miles. You would, however, come back quick in the steamer. Go down stairs and consider the subject carefully, and form your plan complete. Consider how you will manage to get on board the raft, and to get off again ; and where you will stop to take the steamer, and when you will get home ; and when you have planned it all completely, come to me again."

So Rollo went down, and after making various inquiries and calculations, he returned in about ten minutes to Mr. George, with the following plan.

"The waiter tells me," said he, "that the captain of the raft will take me down as far as I want to go, and set me ashore any where, in his boat, for two or three groschen, and that one of the boatmen here will take me out to the raft, when she comes by, for two groschen. A good place for me to stop would be Boppard, which is about ten or twelve miles below here. The raft will get there about two o'clock. Then there will be a steamer coming along by there at three, which will bring up here at four, just about dinner time. The waiter says that he will go out with me to the raft, and explain it all to the captain, because the captain would not understand me, as he only knows German."

"Very well," said Mr. George. "That's a very good plan. Only I advise you to make a bargain with the captain to put you ashore any where you like. Because you know you may get tired before you have gone so far as ten miles.

"In fact," continued Mr. George, "I would not say any thing about the distance that you wish to go to the captain. Just make a bargain with him to let you go aboard his raft for a little while, and to send you ashore whenever you wish to go."

"Yes," said Rollo, "I will; that will be the best plan. But I am sure that I shall want to go as far as ten miles."

So Rollo went to his trunk, and began to unlock it in a hurried manner ; and when he had opened it, he put his hand down into it at the left hand corner, on the front side, which was the place where he always kept his fishing line.

"What are you looking for?" said Mr. George.

"My fishing line," replied Rollo ; "is not that a good plan ? "

"Yes," said Mr. George, "an excellent plan."

Rollo had no very definite idea of being able to fish while on the raft, but there was a sort of instinct which prompted him always to take his fishing line whenever he went on any excursion whatever that was connected with the water. Mr. George had a pretty definite idea that he would *not* be able to fish ; but still he thought it a good plan for Rollo to take the line, for he observed that to have a fishing line in his pocket, on such occasions, was always a source of pleasure to a boy, even if he did not use it at all.

Rollo, having found his fishing line, shut and locked his trunk, and ran down stairs.

As soon as he had gone, Mr. George rose and rang the bell.

Very soon the waiter came to the door.

"This young gentleman who is with me," said Mr. George, "wishes to go on board this raft, and sail down the river a little way."

"Yes, sir," said the waiter. "Rudolf is arranging it for him."

"Very well," said Mr. George. "And now I wish to have you send a commissioner secretly to accompany him. The commissioner is to remain on the raft as long as Rollo does, and leave it when he leaves it, and keep in sight of him all the time till he gets home, so as to see that he does not get into any difficulty."

"Yes, sir," said the waiter.

"But let the commissioner understand that he is not to let Rollo know any thing about his having any charge over him, nor to communicate with him in any way, unless some emergency should arise requiring him to interpose."

"Yes, sir," said the waiter, "I will explain it to him."

"And choose a good-natured and careful man to send," continued Mr. George ; "one that speaks French."

"Yes, sir," replied the waiter ; and so saying, he disappeared, leaving Mr. George to go on with his writing.

In the mean time Rollo had gone down to the shore with the waiter Rudolf, and was standing there near a boat which was drawn up at the foot of the landing stairs, watching the raft, which was now getting pretty near. There was a great company of men at each end of the raft. Rollo could see those at the lowest end the plainest. They were standing in rows near the end of the raft, and every six of them had an oar. There were eight or ten of these oars, all projecting forward, from the front end of the raft, and the

raftsmen, by working them, seemed to be endeav-
oring to row that end of the raft out farther into
the stream. It was the same at the farther end
of the raft. There was a similar number of oars-
men there, and of oars, only those projected behind, just as the others did before. There were
no oars at all along the sides of the raft.

The fact is, that these monstrous rafts are always allowed to float down by the current, the
men not attempting to hasten them on their way
by rowing. All that they attempt to do by their
labor is to keep the immense and unwieldy mass
in the middle of the stream. Thus they only
need oars at the two ends, and the working of
them only tends to row the raft sidewise, as it
were. Sometimes they have to row the ends from
left to right, and sometimes from right to left,
according as the current tends to drift the raft
towards the left or the right bank of the river.

Rollo did not understand this at first, and accordingly, when he first saw these rafts coming
with a dense crowd of men at each end, rowing
vigorously, while there was not a single oar to be
seen, nor even any place for an oar along the
sides, he was very much surprised at the spectacle. He thought that the men at the back end
of the raft were sculling ; but what those at the
forward end were doing he could not imagine.

When, however, he came to consider the case, he saw what the explanation must be, and so he understood the subject perfectly.

At length, when Rollo saw that the forward end of the raft, in its progress down the river, had come nearly opposite to the place where he was standing, he got into the boat, and the boat-man rowed him out to the raft. As soon as they reached the raft Rollo stepped out upon the boards and logs. The top of the raft made a very good and smooth floor, being covered with boards, and it was high and dry above the water. Rollo looked down into the interstices, and saw that that part of the raft which was under water was formed of logs and timbers of very large size, placed close together side by side, with a layer above crossing the layer below. The whole was then covered with a flooring of boards, so close and continuous that Rollo had to look for some time before he could find any openings where he could look down and see how the raft was constructed.

In the middle of the raft were several houses. The houses were made of boards, and were of the plainest and simplest construction. Around the doors of these houses several women were sitting wherever they could find shady places. Some were knitting and some were sewing.

There were several children there too, amusing themselves in various ways. One was skipping a rope. Rudolf conducted Rollo up to one of these families, and told the women that he was an American boy, who was travelling with his uncle on the Rhine, and seeing this raft going by, had a curiosity to come on board of it. The women looked very much pleased when they heard this. Some of them had friends in America, and others were thinking of going themselves with their husbands; and they immediately began to talk very volubly to Rollo, and to ask him questions. But as they spoke German, Rollo could not under stand what they said.

In the mean time the waiter had gone away to speak to the captain of the raft, and to make arrangements for having Rollo put ashore when he had sailed long enough upon it. The captain was walking to and fro, upon a raised platform, near the middle of the raft. This platform I will de-scribe presently. In a few minutes the man re-turned.

"The captain gives you a good welcome," said he, "and says he wishes he could talk English, for he wants to ask you a great many questions about America. He says you may stay on the raft as long as you please, and when you wish to go ashore, you have only to go and get on board one of the boats, and that will be a signal. He will soon see you there, and will send a man to row you to the shore."

Rollo liked this plan very much. So Rudolf, having arranged every thing, wished Rollo a "good voyage," and went off in the boat as he came.

Thus Rollo was left alone, as it were, upon the raft ; and for a moment he felt a little appalled at the idea of going down through such a dark and gloomy gorge as the bed of the river here presented to view, on such a strange conveyance, and surrounded with so wild and savage a horde of men as the raftsmen were, — especially since, as he supposed, there was not a human being on board with whom he could exchange a word of conversation. It is true the commissioner whom his uncle George had sent was on the raft. He had come out in the same boat with Rollo, and had remained when the boat went back to the shore. But Rollo had not noticed him particularly. He observed, it is true, that two men came with him to the raft, and that only one returned ; but he thought it probable that the other might be going down the river a little way, or perhaps that he belonged to the raft. He had not the least idea that the man had come to take charge of *him*, and so he felt as if he were entirely alone in the new and strange scene to which he found himself so suddenly transferred.

There were, however, so many things to attract his attention that at first he had no time to think much of his loneliness. There was a fire burning at a certain part of the raft, not far from the dooi of one of the houses, and he went to see it. As soon as he reached it, the mystery in respect to the means of having a fire on such a structure, without setting the boards and timbers on fire, was at once solved. Rollo found that the fire was built upon a hearth of *sand*. There was a large box, about four feet square and a foot deep, which box was filled with sand, and the fire was built in the middle of it. It seemed to Rollo that this was a very easy way to make a fireplace, especially as the sand seemed to be of a very common kind, such as the raftsmen had probably shovelled up somewhere on the shore of the river.

"The very next time I build a raft," said Rollo, "I will have a fire on it in exactly that way."

There was a sort of barricade or screen built up on two sides of this fire, to keep the wind from blowing the flame and the heat away from the kettle that was hung over it. This screen was made of short boards, nailed to three posts.

The captain's station on the raft.

that were placed in such a manner as to make, when the boards were nailed to them, two short fences, at right angles to each other, or like two sides of a high box. The corner of this screen was turned towards the wind, and thus the fire was sheltered. A pole passed across from one of the posts to the other, and the kettle was hung upon the pole.

After examining this fireplace Rollo went to look at the platform where the captain had his station. This platform was about six feet high and ten feet long ; and it was just wide enough for the captain to walk to and fro upon it. There was a flight of steps leading up to this platform from the floor of the raft, and a little railing on each side of it, to keep the captain from falling off while he was walking there.

The object of having this platform raised in this way, was to give the captain a more commanding position, so as not only to enable him to survey the whole of the raft, and observe how every thing was going on upon it, but also to give him a good view of the river below, so that he might watch the currents, and see how the raft was drifting, and give the necessary orders for working it one way or the other, as might be required in order to keep it in the middle of the stream.

Then Rollo went to the forward end of the raft to see the raftsmen row. The oars were of monstrous size, as you might well suppose to be the case from the fact that each of them required six men to work it. These six men all stood in a row along the handle of the oar, which seemed to be as large as a small mast. They all pressed down upon the handle of the oar so as to raise the blade out of the water, and then walked along over the floor of the raft quite a considerable distance. At last they stopped, and lifting up their hands, they allowed the blade of the oar to go down into the water. Then they turned, and began to push the oar with their hands the other way. The outside men had to reach up very high, for as the oar was very long, and the blade was now necessarily in the water, the end of the handle was raised quite high in the air. The men, accordingly, that were nearest the end of the oar, were obliged to hold their hands up high, in order to reach it ; and they all walked along very deliberately, like a platoon of soldiers, pushing the oar before them as they advanced. And as each of the other six oars had a similar platoon marching with it to and fro, and as all acted in concert, and kept time with each other in their motions, the whole operation had quite the appearance of a military manœuvre. Rollo watched it for some time with great satisfaction.

After this Rollo walked up and down the raft two or three times, and then his attention was attracted by a steamer going by. The steamer cut her way through the water with great speed, and the waves made by her paddle wheels dashed up against the margin of the raft as if it had been along shore.

There was a great number of tourists on board the steamer. Rollo could see them very distinctly sitting under the awning on the deck. Some were standing by the railing and examining the raft by means of their spy glasses or opera glasses. Others were seated at tables, eating late breakfasts, in little parties by themselves. The boat glided by very swiftly, however, and soon Rollo could see nothing of her but the stern, and the foaming wake which her paddle wheels left behind them in the water.

As soon as the steamboat had gone by, Rollo began to feel a slight sense of loneliness on the raft, which feeling was increased by the sombre aspect of the scenery around him. The river was closely shut in by mountains on both sides, and between them the raft seemed to be drifting slowly down into a dark and gloomy gorge, which, though it might have seemed simply sublime to

162   ROLLO ON THE RHINE.

Rollo concludes he does not want to go all the way to Boppard.

a pleasant party viewing it together from the cheerful deck of a steamer, or from a comfortable carriage on the banks, was well fitted to awaken an emotion of awe and terror in the mind of a boy like Rollo, floating down into it helplessly on an enormous raft, with a hundred men, looking more like brigands than any thing else, marching solemnly to and fro at either end of it, working prodigious oars, with incessant toil, to prevent its being carried upon the rocks and dashed to pieces. In fact, Rollo began soon to wish that he was safe on shore again.

"I am very thankful," said he to himself, "that I made a bargain with the captain to put me ashore whenever I wished to go. I don't believe that I shall wish to go more than half way to Boppard."

So saying, Rollo looked anxiously down the river. The mountains looked more and more dark and gloomy, and they appeared to shut in before him in such a manner that he could not see how it could be possible for such an immense raft to twist its way through between them.

"I don't believe I shall wish to go more than a quarter of the way to Boppard," said he.

Two or three minutes afterwards, on looking back, he saw the town of St. Goar, where he had embarked, gradually disappearing behind a

ROLLO ON THE RAFT.

wooded promontory which was slowly coming in the way, and cutting it off from view.

"In fact," said Rollo to himself, "since I am not going all the way to Boppard, I had better not go much farther; for I shall have to walk back, as the steamer does not stop this side of Boppard. Besides, I have seen all that there is on the raft already, and there is no use in staying on it any longer."

So he concluded to go at once to the boat, according to the arrangement which he had made with the captain. He was afraid that he might have to wait some time before the captain would see him; but he did not. The captain saw him immediately, and sent a man to row him ashore. *Two* men came. in fact, the commissioner being one of them. But Rollo did not pay any particular attention to this circumstance. He did not even observe that it was the same man that had come on board with him. Rollo could not talk to the oarsman on the way, but on landing he gave him a little money, — about what he thought was proper, — and then went up into the road with a view to go home. The commissioner, in order not to awaken any suspicions in Rollo's mind that he was following him, turned away as soon as he landed, and walked along the tow path. down the stream.

Rollo went slowly home. He had not been more than half an hour on the raft. and had not gone down the stream more than a mile ; so that in three quarters of an hour after he had left his uncle at the hotel he found himself drawing near to it again, on his return.

He felt a little ashamed to get back so soon. So he thought that he would not go in at once and report himself to his uncle, but would go down on the bank of the river, and see if he could find a place to fish a little while, until some little time should have elapsed, so as to give to the period of his absence a tolerably respectable duration. "Uncle George will laugh at me," said he to himself, "if he sees me come home so soon."

So Rollo went down to the quay, and taking out his fishing line, he began to make arrangements for fishing. He did not, however, feel quite at his ease. There seemed to be something a little like artifice in thus prolonging his absence in order to make his uncle think that he had gone farther down the river than he had been. It was not being quite honest, he thought.

"After all," said he to himself, "I'll go and tell uncle George now. I shall have a better time fishing if I do. If he chooses to laugh at

me, he may. If he is going to do it, I should like
to have it over."

So he went into the hotel, and advanced some
what timidly to the door of the room where he
had left his uncle writing. He opened the door,
and looking in, said, —

" Uncle George! I've got back."

Mr. George did not seem at all surprised, but
looking up a moment from his writing, he smiled,
and said, —

" Ah! I'm glad to see you safe back again.
It is rather lonesome here without you. Did you
have a pleasant voyage?"

" Yes," said Rollo, " very pleasant. Only I
did not go very far. I got them to put me ashore
about a mile below here."

" That was right," said Mr. George. " You did
exactly as I should have done myself. In fact
you can see all you wish to see on such a raft in
half an hour."

" Yes," said Rollo, " I found that I could."

" And I am very glad that you came to tell
me," said Mr. George, " as soon as you came
home."

So Rollo, quite relieved in mind, went down
stairs again, and returning to the quay, he re
sumed his fishing.

CHAPTER XII.

DINNER.

ABOUT half past three o'clock Rollo went up to his uncle's room.

"Uncle George," said he, "have not you got almost through with your writing?"

"Why," said Mr. George, "are you tired of staying here?"

"Yes," said Rollo, "I am tired of being down in the bottom of such a deep valley. I wish you would put away your writing and go on up the river till we get out where we can see, and then you may write as much as you please."

"Do you wish to go up the river to-night?" asked Mr. George.

"Yes," said Rollo, "very much."

Mr. George took out his watch.

"Go down and ask the waiter when the next steamer comes along."

Rollo went down, and presently returned with the report that the next steamer came by at five o'clock.

" There is a place up the river about two hours' sail, called Bingen," said Mr. George, " where the mountains end. Above that the country is open and level, and the river wide. We might go up there, I suppose; but what should we do for dinner ? "

" We might have dinner on board the steamer," said Rollo.

" Very well," said Mr. George ; " that's what we will do. You may go and tell the waiter to bring me the bill, and then be ready at half past four. That will give me an hour more to write."

At half past four Rollo came to tell Mr. George that the steamer was coming. The trunk had been previously carried down and put on board a small boat, for this was one of the places where the steamers were not accustomed to come up to a pier, but received and landed passengers by means of small boats that went out to meet them in the middle of the river. Such a boat was now ready at the foot of the landing stairs, and Mr. George and Rollo got into it.

The boatman waited until the steamer came pretty near, and then he rowed out to meet it. He stopped rowing when the boat was opposite to the paddle wheel of the steamer, and the

steamer stopped her engine at the same time.
A man who stood on the paddle box threw
a rope to the boat, and the boatman made
this rope fast to a belaying pin that was set for
the purpose near the bow of the boat. By means
of this rope the boat was then drawn rapidly up
alongside the steamer, at a place directly aft
the paddle wheel, where there was a little stairway above, and a small platform below, both of
which, when not in use, were drawn up out of the
way, but which were always let down when passengers were to come on board. As soon as the
boat came alongside this apparatus, Rollo and
Mr. George stepped out upon the platform, and
went up the little stairway, the hands on board
the steamer standing there to help them. In a
moment more the trunk was passed up, the boat
was pushed off, and the paddle wheels of the
steamer were put in motion; and thus, almost
before Rollo had time to think what was going
on, he found himself comfortably seated on a
camp stool under the awning, by the side of Mr.
George, on the quarter deck of the steamer,
and sailing swiftly along on his voyage up the
river.

"What sudden transitions we pass through,"
said Mr. George, "in travelling on the Rhine!"

"Yes," said Rollo, "it seems scarcely five

minutes ago that I was sitting, all by myself, on the bank of a lonesome river, fishing ; and now I am on board a steamer, with all this company, and dashing away through the water at a great rate."

"True," said Mr. George ; "and how quickly we came on board! One minute we are creeping along slowly over the water in a little boat, and the next, as if by some sort of magic, we find ourselves on the deck of the steamer, with the boat drifting away astern."

"How high the mountains are," said Rollo, "along the shores here! Do the mountains end at Bingen ? "

"Yes," said Mr. George, " at Bingen, or soon after that. There the country opens, and the banks of the river become level and flat. The river widens, and there are a great many islands in it. There we come to railroads again too, for where the land is level they can make railroads very easily. It would be very difficult to make a railroad here, though I believe they are going to do it."

"I should think it would be difficult," said Rollo. "But now, uncle George, about our dinner."

"Very well," said Mr. George, "about the dinner." So the two travellers held a consultation on this subject, and concluded what to have

A few minutes afterwards a waiter came by, carrying a large salver, with some coffee and bread and butter upon it, for a gentleman on the deck. Mr. George beckoned to this waiter, and when he came to him, he ordered the dinner that he and Rollo had agreed upon. It consisted of sausages for Rollo, a beefsteak for Mr. George, and fried potatoes for both. After that they were to have an omelet and some coffee. The coffee on board the Rhine steamers, being made with very rich and pure milk, is delicious.

The waiter brought up a small square table to the part of the deck where Mr. George and Rollo were sitting, which was under the shady side of the awning, and set it for their dinner. In about twenty minutes the dinner was ready. The table itself was as neat and nice as possible, and the dishes which had been ordered were prepared in the most perfect manner. I need not add, I suppose, that Mr. George and Rollo — it being now so late — were provided with excellent appetites. So they had a very good time eating their dinner. While they were eating it they could watch the changes in the scenery of the banks, as they glided swiftly along, and observe the steamers, tow boats, and other river craft that passed them from time to time.

While they were at dinner, Rollo asked Mr.

George about the rafts, and where the timber that they were made of came from.

DINNER ON THE RHINE.

"Why, you see," said Mr. George, "the River Rhine, in the upper portions of it, has a great many branches which come down from among the mountains, where nothing will grow well but timber. So they reserve these places for forests, and as fast as the timber gets grown, they cut it down, and slide it down the slopes to the nearest stream, and then float it along till they come to great streams ; and there they form it into rafts, and send it down the river to Holland and Belgium, where timber does not grow."

"Would not timber grow in Belgium and Holland ?" asked Rollo.

"Yes," said Mr. George, "it would grow very well, but the land is too valuable to appropriate it to such a purpose. The whole country below Cologne, where we came to the river, is smooth and level, and free from stones, so that it is easily ploughed and tilled ; and thus grain, and flax, and other very valuable crops can be raised upon it. They raise a few trees in that part of the country, but not many."

"I never heard of raising trees before," said Rollo, "except apple trees, or something like that."

"True," said Mr. George, "because in America, as that is a new country, there is an abundance of native forests, where the trees grow wild. But you must remember that every foot of land in Europe has been in the possession of man, and occupied by him, for two thousand years. There

is not a field or a hill, or even a rocky steep on
the mountain side, which has not had sixty or
seventy generations of owners, who have all been
watching it, and taking care of it, and improving
it more or less all that time ; each one carefully
considering what his land can produce most
profitably, and taking care of it and managing it
especially with reference to that production. If
his land is smooth and level, he ploughs it, and
cultivates it for grass, or grain, or other plants
requiring special tillage. If it is in steep slopes,
with a warm exposure, he terraces it up, and
makes vineyards of it. If it is in steep slopes,
with a cold exposure, then it will do for timber,
provided there are streams near it, so that he can
float the timber away. If there are no streams
near it, he can use it as pasture ground for sheep
or cattle ; for the wool, or the butter and cheese,
which he obtains from this kind of farming, can
be transported without streams ; or, at least, such
commodities will bear transporting farther before coming to a stream than wood or timber.
Thus, you see, whatever the land is fit for, it has
been appropriated to for a great many centuries ;
and it has all been cropped over and over
again, even where the crop is a forest of trees.
If we allow the trees even a hundred years
to grow, before they are large enough to cut

that would give, in two thousand years, time to cut them off and let them grow up again twenty times."

" Here comes a steamer," said Rollo.

Just then the bow of a steamer came shooting into view, down the river. On the forward part of the deck were several soldiers and laborers, with women and children that looked like emigrants, and also a .huge pile of trunks and merchandise covered with a tarpauling. Then came the paddle wheels, and then the quarter deck, with a large company of tourists, most of whom were looking about very eagerly at the scenery, with guide books and glasses in their hands. These were tourists that had been travelling in Switzerland, and were coming home by way of the Rhine ; and as they were now just entering the part of the river where the grand and imposing scenery was to be seen, — though Mr. George and Rollo were just leaving it, — they were full of wonder and admiration at the various objects which appeared around them on every side. Rollo had but a very brief opportunity to look at these strangers, for the steamer which conveyed them passed by very swiftly, and in a moment they were gone.

" How swift ! " said Rollo.

" Yes," said Mr. George, " they go down the

stream much faster than they go up; for in going down they have the current to help them, but we have it to hinder us in going up."

"And does it help just as much as it hinders?" asked Rollo.

"Yes," said Mr. George, "for any given time. If the current flows two miles an hour, it will carry forward a boat that is going *with* it just two miles faster than it would go in still water. And if the boat is going *against* it, it will go just two miles an hour slower.

"Thus, you see," continued **Mr. George**, "if a steamer had an engine capable of driving her twelve miles an hour through the water, in navigating a stream that flows *two* miles an hour, she would go *fourteen* miles an hour in going down, and *ten* miles an hour in going up."

"Then," said Rollo, "it seems that the *help* of a current is just as much as the *hinderance* of it, and that a river running fast is just as good for navigation as if the water were still. Because, you see," he added, "that though they lose some headway in going up, they gain it just the same in coming down."

"That reasoning seems plausible," replied **Mr. George**, "but it is not sound."

"What do you mean by *plausible?*" asked Rollo.

"Why, it *appears* to be good, when it really is not so. Reasoning very often appears to be good, while there is all the time some latent flaw in it which makes the conclusion wrong. Very often something is left out of the account which ought to be taken in and calculated for, and that is the case here. The truth is, that the current helps the steamer in going down just as much as it retards her in coming up *for any given time;* as for instance, for an hour, or for six hours. But we are to consider that in accomplishing any given *distance,* the steamer is longer in coming up than she is in going down, and so is exposed to the retarding effect of the current longer than she has the benefit of its coöperation.

"For example," continued Mr. George, "suppose the distance from one place to another, on a river flowing two miles an hour, is such that it takes a steamer three hours to go down and four hours to come up. In going down she would be aided how much?"

"Two miles an hour," said Rollo.

"And that makes how much for the whole time going down?" asked Mr. George.

"Six miles," said Rollo.

"Now, it takes her *four* hours to go up," said Mr. George. "How much would she be kept back then by the current?"

Steamers and rafts.   There is much to come down — little to go up.

" Why, two miles an hour for *four* hours," said Rollo, " which would make eight miles."

" Thus in the double voyage," said Mr. George, " the boat would be helped *six* miles and hindered *eight*, so that the current would on the whole be a serious disadvantage. For a steamer, there- fore, which is to be navigated equally both ways, the current is an evil.

"But for that sort of navigation which goes only one way, it is a great advantage. For in- stance, the rafts have to come down, but they never have to go back again ; and so they have the whole advantage of the current in bringing them down, without any disadvantage to bal- ance it.

" On the whole," said Mr. George, " I do not see but that the currents of great rivers are an advantage, for there is always a much greater quantity to come down than to go up. The heavy products that grow on the borders of the rivers are to come down, while comparatively little in quantity goes up. So the benefit, on the whole, which is produced by the flow of the water, may be greater than the injury."

" What do they do with the rafts," said Rollo, " when they get them down the river ? "

" They break them up," said Mr. George, " and sell the timber in the countries near the mouth of the river, where but little timber grows."

By this time, Mr. George and Rollo had finished eating the meats which they had ordered for their dinner, and so the waiter came and took away the plates, and brought the omelet and the coffee. With the coffee the waiter brought two small plates and knives, and some very nice rolls and butter. He also brought a plate containing several slices of a kind of cake, *toasted*. This cake was very nice.

While Rollo was eating it he asked his uncle George whether, in case he had gone down the river to Boppard, and had not got back until dark, he should not have been anxious about him.

" No," said Mr. George, " not much. I took precautions against that."

" What precautions? " asked Rollo.

" Why, I sent a man with you to take care of you," said Mr. George.

" You sent a man with me ? " repeated Rollo, very much surprised.

" Yes," said Mr. George, quietly. " As soon as you had gone out of my room, to go on board the raft, I called the waiter, and asked him to send a commissioner with you, to see that you did not get into any difficulty, and to take care of you in case there should be any occasion."

"Now, uncle George," said Rollo, in a mourn-ful and complaining tone, "that was not fair."

"Why not?" asked Mr. George.

"Because," said Rollo, "I wanted to take care of myself."

"Well," said Mr. George, "you *did* take care of yourself — didn't you? My plan did not inter-fere with yours at all — did it?"

Rollo did not answer, but he ooked as if he were not convinced.

"I gave the man special charge," said Mr. George, "not to interfere with you in any way, and not even to let you know that I had said any thing about you to him, so that you should be left entirely to your own resources. And you *were* so left. You acted in the whole affair just as you thought proper, and took care of yourself admirably well. I think especially that you were very wise in leaving the raft when you did, instead of remaining on board three or four hours longer. But however this may be, you acted for yourself throughout. I did not inter-fere with you at all."

"Well," said Rollo, after a moment's pause, "what you say is very true. But it seems to me it was a little artful in you to do that; and you always tell me that I must not be art-ful, but must be perfectly honest and open in

all that I do. Don't you think you deceived
me a little ? "

" I do not see that I did," said Mr. George.
" When we deceive a person, we do it by saying
or doing something to give him a false impression, or to make him suppose that something is
true which is not true. Now, what did I do or
say to give you any false impression ? "

" Why, nothing, I suppose," said Rollo, " except
sending that man to take care of me without
letting me know it."

" That was *concealing* something from you,"
said Mr. George, " not deceiving you. There
are a thousand occasions when it is right to conceal things from the people around us. That is
very different from deceiving them. This was a
case in which I thought it best to conceal what I
did, for a time, though I intended to tell you in
the end. You see, I should not have done my
duty, as a guardian intrusted with the care of a
boy by his father, if I had allowed you to go
away from me on such a doubtful expedition
without some precautions. So I thought it best
to send the commissioner ; but I knew you wished
to take care of yourself, and so I charged the
commissioner to allow you to do so, and on no
account to interpose, unless some accident, or un-
foreseen emergency, should occur. I told him not

even to let you know that he was there, so that you might not be embarrassed or restricted at all by his presence, or even relieved of any por-tion of your solicitude. But I determined to tell you all about it as soon as it was over, and I was fondly imagining that you would praise me for my sagacity in managing the business as I did, and also especially for my openness and honesty in explaining all to you at last. But in-stead of that, it seems you think I did wrong ; so that where I expected compliments and praise, I get only censure and condemnation ; and I do not know what I shall do."

Mr. George said this with a perfectly grave face, and with such a tone of mock meekness and despondency, that Rollo burst into a loud laugh.

"If you could think of any suitable punish-ment for me," continued Mr. George, in the same penitent tone, "I would submit to it very con-tentedly ; though I do not see myself any suitable way by which I can be punished, except perhaps by a fine."

"Yes," said Rollo, "a fine ; you shall be fined, uncle George. There is a woman out here that has got some raspberries, in little paper baskets. You shall be fined a paper of rasp-berries."

Mr. George acceded to this proposal. The raspberries were two groschen a basket. Mr. George gave Rollo the money, and Rollo, going forward with it, bought the raspberries, and he and Mr. George ate them up together. They served the double purpose of a punishment for the offence, and of a dessert for the dinner.

The piers on the Rhine are not solid, but floating piers.

CHAPTER XIII.

BINGEN.

AT some places on the Rhine the passengers go on board the steamers and land from them in a small boat, as Mr. George and Rollo did at St. Goar. At others there is a regular pier for a landing. At all the large towns there is a pier, — in some there are two or three, — which belong severally to the different companies which own the lines of steamers. These piers are constructed in a very peculiar manner. They are made by means of a large and heavy boat, which is anchored at a short distance from the shore, and then a massive platform is built, extending from the quay to this boat. The boat, being afloat, rises and falls with the river ; and thus the end of the platform which rests upon it is kept always at the proper level for the landing of the passengers, so that, whatever may be the state of the water, they go over on a level plank. This is a very convenient arrangement for such a river as the Rhine, which rises and falls considerably at different seasons, on account of the variation in the quantity of rain, and in the melting of the snows, on the mountains in Switzerland.

Bingen is one of the towns where there is a floating pier of this kind, and Mr. George and Rollo were safely landed upon it about eight o'clock. It was a very pleasant evening. As they approached the town, before they landed, they both walked forward towards the bows of the vessel, to see what sort of a place it was where they were going to spend the night.

"It is just like Coblenz," said Mr. George, "only on a small scale."

It was indeed very much like Coblenz in its situation, for it was built on a point of land formed between the Rhine and the Nahe, a branch which came in here from the westward, just as Coblenz was at the junction of the Rhine and the Moselle. There was a bridge across the Moselle, you recollect, just at the mouth of it, on the lower side of the town, which bridge was made to accommodate the travellers going up and down the Rhine on that side. There was just such a bridge across the mouth of the Nahe. So that the situation of the town was in all respects very similar to that of Coblenz.

Just below the town there was a small green island covered with shrubbery, and on the upper

end of the island was a high, square tower, stand
ing alone.

" That's must be Bishop Hatto's Tower," said
Mr. George.

" Who was he ? " asked Rollo.

" He was a man that was eaten up by the
rats," said Mr. George, " because he called the
poor people rats, and burned up a great many of
them in his barn. The story is in the guide
book. I will read it to you when we get to the
hotel."

By this time the boat had glided by the island,
and the tower was out of view ; and very soon
afterwards Mr. George and Rollo were landed
on the floating pier, as I have already said.
There were very few people to land, and the boat
seemed merely to touch the pier and then to
glide away again.

There were several porters standing by, and
they immediately took up the passengers' bag-
gage, and carried it away to the hotels, which
were all very near the river. Rollo and Mr.
George were soon comfortably established in a
room with two beds in it, one in each corner, and
a large round table near one of the windows.
Outside of the other window was a balcony,
and Rollo immediately went out there, to look
at the view.

"We have not got quite *out* yet, uncle George," said he.

Rollo was right, for the bank of the river opposite Bingen was very steep and high, and was terraced from top to bottom for vineyards. In fact, this part of the river is more celebrated, perhaps, than any other for the excellent quality of the grapes which it produces. It is here that are situated the famous vineyards of Rudesheim and Johannisberg. In fact, the whole country, for miles in extent, is one vast vineyard. The separate fields are divided from one another by the terrace walls, which run parallel to the river, and by paths formed sometimes by steps, and sometimes by zigzags, which ascend and descend from the crest of the hills above to the line of the shore. The only buildings to be seen among all this vast expanse of walls and terraces are the little watchtowers that are erected here and there at commanding points to enable the vine-growers to watch the fruit, when it comes to the time of ripening. The laborers who till the fields, and dress the vines, and gather the grapes in the season, live all of them in compact villages, built at intervals along the shore.

While Rollo was looking at this scene, and wondering how such an immense number of walls and terraces could ever have been built his attention was suddenly arrested by hearing a sweet and silvery voice, like that of a girl, calling out, —

" Rollo."

Rollo turned in the direction of the sound, and found that it was Minnie speaking to him. She was standing on another balcony, one which opened from the chamber next to his. Rollo was very much pleased to see her. He thought it very remarkable that he should meet her thus so many times; but it was not. Travellers on the Rhine going in the same direction, and stopping to see the same things, often meet each other in this way again and again.

After talking with Minnie some little time from the balcony, Rollo asked her if her mother was there.

" Yes," said Minnie.

" Ask her then," said Rollo, " if you may come down and take a walk with me in the garden."

Minnie went in from the balcony, and in a moment returning, she said, " Yes," and immediately disappeared again. So Rollo went down, and Minnie presently came and met him in the garden.

The garden was a small piece of ground in front of the hotel, between the hotel and the

MINNIE.

river.   There was a large gate opening from it
towards the hotel, and another towards the river

A description of the hotel garden at Bingen.

The garden was full of shade trees, with pleasant walks winding about among them, and here and there a border, or a bed of flowers. There were several carved images placed here and there, one of which amused Rollo and Minnie very much, for it represented a monkey sitting on a pole and looking at himself in a hand looking glass which he held before his face. In the other hand he had a parasol.

In the front part of the garden, towards the river, were several tables under the trees, where people might take coffee or ices, or they might take their dinner there if they chose. In the front of the garden too, at the corners, were two summer houses, with tables and chairs in them. The sides of these houses that were turned towards the river, and also those that were towards the gardens, were open. The other two sides of each summer house had walls, on which were painted views of castles and other scenery of the Rhine. Over one of the summer houses was a little room for a lookout, where there was a very fine prospect up and down the river.

Rollo and Minnie rambled about here for some time, examining every thing with great attention. They chose one of the pleasantest tables, and sat down before it.

"This is a nice place," said Minnie. "I propose that you and I come out here to-morrow morning and have breakfast, all by ourselves."

"O, we can't do that very well," said Rollo.

"Yes we can," replied Minnie, "just as well as not. I'll plan it all."

Minnie then jumped up and led the way, Rollo following, through the open gate towards the river. There was a sort of street outside, and Rollo and Minnie stood here for a few minutes to see a steamer go by. Minnie then proposed that they should get into a boat that was lying there, and take a sail.

"You can row — can't you?" said she to Rollo.

"No," said Rollo, "not on such a river as this. See how swift the current flows."

"Never mind," said Minnie, "I can. Let us jump into this boat, and have a sail."

"No," said Rollo, "not for the world. We should be carried off down the stream in spite of every thing."

"Never mind," said Minnie ; "we should land somewhere, and they would send down for us. We should have a great deal of fun."

How far Minnie would have persevered in urging her plan for a venture in the boat on

Mr. George joins the children.

the river I do not know ; but the conversation was here interrupted by the appearance of Mr. George, who had come down through the garden, and just at this instant joined the children on the quay.

CHAPTER XIV.

THE RUIN IN THE GARDEN.

MR. GEORGE said that he had come to ask Rollo to go and take a walk to see an old ruin in the town, and he told Minnie that he should be very glad to have her go too, if her mother would be willing.

"O, yes," said Minnie, "she will be willing. I'll go."

"You must go and ask her first," said Mr. George.

So, while Mr. George and Rollo walked slowly up towards the hotel, Minnie ran before them to ask her mother.

Mr. George explained to Rollo in walking through the garden, that there were two ruins that he wished to see while he was at Bingen. One was the famous castle of Rheinstein, which stood on the bank of the river, a few miles below the town.

"But it is too late to go there to-night," said Mr. George. "We will take that for to-morrow

Mr. George and the children trying to find their way to the ruins.

But there is an old ruin back here in the village, which I think we can see to-night."

When they reached the door of the hotel, Minnie met them, and said that she could go ; and so they walked along together.

Mr. George groped about a long time among the narrow streets and passage ways of the town, to find some way of access to the ruin, but in vain. He obtained frequent views of it, and of the rocky hill that it stood upon, which was seen here and there, by chance glimpses, rising in massive grandeur above the houses of the town ; but he could not find any way to get to it.

"It is in a private garden," said Mr. George, " I know ; but how to find the way to it I cannot imagine."

" Perhaps it is here," said Minnie.

So saying, Minnie ran up to a gate by the side of the street, which led into a very pretty yard, all shaded with trees and shrubbery, and having a large and handsome house by the side of it. The gate was shut and fastened, but Minnie could look through the bars.

There was a woman standing near one of the doors of the house, and Minnie beckoned to her. The woman came immediately down towards the gate. Minnie pointed in towards a walk which seemed to lead back among the trees, and said to the woman, —

" *Schloss ?* "

Schloss is the German word for *castle*. Minnie could not speak German; but she knew some words of that language, and the words that she did know she was always perfectly ready to use, whenever an occasion presented.

" *Ja, Ja,*" said the woman; and immediately she opened the gate. By this time Minnie had beckoned Mr. George and Rollo to come up from the road, and they all three went in through the gate.

The woman called to a man who was then just coming down out of the garden, and said something to him in German. None of our party could understand what she said; but they knew from the circumstances of the case, and from her actions, that she was saying to him that the strangers wished to see the ruins. So, the man leading the way, and the three visitors following him, they all went on along a broad gravel walk which led up into the garden.

Mr. George asked the guide if he could speak English, and he said, " *Nein.*" Then he asked him if he could speak French, and he said, " *Nein.*" He said he could only speak German.

"He can't explain any thing to us, children,'

said Mr. George ; "we shall have to judge for ourselves."

The walk was very shady that led along the garden, and as it was now long past eight o'clock, it was nearly dark walking there, though it was still pretty light under the open sky. The walk gradually ascended, and it soon brought the party to a place where they could see, rising up among the trees, fragments of ancient walls of stupendous height. Rollo looked up to them with wonder. He even felt a degree of awe, as well as wonder, for the strange and uncouth forms of windows and doors, which were seen here and there ; the embrasures, and the yawning arches which appeared below, leading apparently to subterranean dungeons, being all dimly seen in the obscurity of the night, suggested to his mind ideas of prisoners confined there in ancient times, and wearing out their lives in a dreadful and hopeless captivity, or being put to death by horrid tortures.

Minnie was still more afraid of these gloomy remains than Rollo. She was afraid to look up at them.

" Look up there, Minnie," said Rollo. "See that old broken window with iron gratings in the walls."

" No," replied Minnie, " I do not want to see it at all."

So saying she looked straight down upon the path before her, and walked on as fast as possible.

"If I should look up there, I should see some dreadful thing mowing and chowing at me," she added.

Rollo laughed, and they all walked on.

Presently the path began to ascend more rapidly, and soon it brought the whole party out into the light, on the slope of an elevation which was covered with the main body of the ruined castle. The man led the way up a steep path, and then up a flight of ancient stone steps built against a wall, until he came to an iron gateway. This he unlocked, and the whole party went in, or rather went through, for as the roofs were gone from the ruins, they were almost as much out of doors after passing through the gateway as they were before.

Mr. George and the children gazed around upon the confused mass of ruined bastions, towers, battlements, and archways, that lay before them, with a feeling of awe which it is impossible to describe. The grass waved and flowers bloomed on the tops of the walls, on the sills of the windows, and on every projecting cornice, or angle, where a seed could have lodged. In many places thick clusters of herbage were seen growing luxuriantly from crumbling interstices of the stones in the perpendicular face of the masonry, fifty feet from the ground. Large trees were growing on what had formerly been the floors of the halls, or of the chambers, and tall grass waved there, ready for the scythe.

There was one tower which still had a roof upon it. A steep flight of stone steps led up to a door in this tower. The door was under a deep archway. The guide led the way up this stairway, and unlocking the door, admitted his party into the tower.

They found themselves, when they had entered, in a small, square room. It occupied the whole extent of the tower on that story, and yet it was very small. This room was in good condition, having been carefully preserved, and was now the only remaining room of the whole castle which was not dismantled and in ruins. But this room, though still shut in from the weather; and protected in a measure from further decay, presented an appearance of age wholly indescribable. The door where the party had come in was on one side of it, and there was a window on the opposite side, leading out to a little stone balcony. On the other two sides were two antique cabinets of carved oak, most aged and venerable in appearance, and of the most quaint

200   ROLLO ON THE RHINE.

The trap door.   Prison.   Minnie does not like ruins.

construction. The walls and the floor were ot stone. In the middle of the floor, however, was a heavy trap door. The guide lifted up this door by means of a ponderous ring of rusty iron, and let Mr. George and the children look down. It was a dark and dismal dungeon.

"*Prison*," said the guide.

This, it seemed, was the only English word that he could speak.

"Yes," said Mr. George, speaking to Rollo and Minnie. "He means that this was the prison of the castle."

The guide shut down the trap door, and the children, after gazing around upon the room a few minutes longer, were glad to go away.

Just before reaching the hotel on their way home, Rollo told Minnie that he and Mr. George were going down the next day to see Rheinstein, a beautiful castle down the river, and he asked her if she would not like to go too.

Mr. George was walking on before them at this time, and he did not hear this conversation.

"No," said Minnie, "I believe not. It makes me afraid to go and see these old ruins."

"But this one that we are going to see is not an old ruin," said Rollo. "It has been all made over again as good as new, and is full of beautiful rooms and beautiful furniture. Besides, it

Minnie's inconsistency

stands out in a good clear place on the bank
of the river, and you will not be afraid at all.
I mean to ask uncle George if I may ask you
to go."

That evening, in reflecting on the adventures
of the day, Rollo wondered that Minnie, who
seemed to have so much courage about going out
in a boat on the water, and in clambering about
into all sorts of dangerous places, should be so
afraid of old ruins ; but the fact is, that people
are in nothing more inconsistent than in their
fears.

202   ROLLO ON THE RHINE.

The invitation to Minnie.   Mr. George's permission.

CHAPTER XV.

RHEINSTEIN.

ROLLO determined to ask his uncle George at breakfast if he might invite Minnie to accompany them on their visit to the castle of Rheinstein. He was sorry, however, when he came to reflect a little, that he had not first asked his uncle George, before mentioning the subject to Minnie at all.

"For," said he to himself, "if there *should* be any difficulty or objection to prevent her going with us, then I shall have to go and tell her that I can't invite her, after all; and that would be worse than not to have said any thing about it."

When, at length, Rollo and Mr. George were seated at table at breakfast, Rollo asked his uncle if he was willing that Minnie should go with them to the castle.

"I told her," said he, "last night, that we were going, and I said I intended to ask you if she might go with us. But I thought afterwards that it would have been better to have spoken about it to you first."

" Yes," said Mr. George, " that would be much the best mode generally, though in this case it makes no difference, for I shall be very glad to have Minnie go."

So Rollo immediately after breakfast went to renew his invitation to Minnie, and about an hour afterwards the party set out on their excursion. They went in a fine open barouche with two horses, which Mr. George selected from several that were standing near the hotel, waiting to be hired. Mr. George took the back seat, and Rollo and Minnie sat together on the front seat. Thus they rode through the streets of the town, and over the old stone bridge which led across the Nahe near its junction with the Rhine.

From the bridge Rollo could see the little green island on which stood Bishop Hatto's Tower.

" There is Bishop Hatto's Tower," said Rollo, " and you promised, uncle George, to tell me the story of it."

" Well," said Mr. George, " I will tell it to you now."

So Mr. George began to relate the story as follows : —

" There was a famine coming on at one time during Bishop Hatto's life, and the people were

becoming very destitute, though the bishop's gran
aries were well supplied with corn. The poor
flocked and crowded around his door. At last
the bishop appointed a time when, he told them,
they should have food for the winter, if they
would repair to his great barn. Young and old,
from far and near, did so, and when the barn
could hold no more, he made fast the door, and
set fire to it, and burned them all. He then returned to his palace, congratulating himself that
the country was rid of the 'rats,' as he called
them. He ate a good supper, went to bed, and
slept like an innocent man ; but he never slept
again. In the morning, when he entered a room
where hung his picture, he found it entirely eaten
by rats. Presently a man came and told him
that the rats had entirely consumed his corn ; and
while the man was telling him this, another man
came running, pale as death, to tell him that ten
thousand rats were coming. 'I'll go to my
tower on the Rhine,' said the bishop ; ''tis the
safest place in Germany.' He immediately hastened to the shore, and crossed to his tower, and
very carefully barred all the doors and windows.
After he had retired for the night, he had hardly
closed his eyes, when he heard a fearful scream.
He started up, and saw the cat sitting by his pillow, screaming with fear of the army of rats

that were approaching. They had swum over the river, climbed the shore, and were scaling the walls of his tower by thousands. The bishop, half dead with fright, fell on his knees, and began counting his beads. The rats soon gained the room, fell upon the bishop, and in a short time nothing was left of him but his bones.

"There is an account of it in poetry too, in my book," said Mr. George.

"Read it to us," said Minnie.

So Mr. George opened his book, and rea 1 the account in poetry, as follows : —

BISHOP HATTO.

The summer and autumn had been so wet,
That in winter the corn was growing yet;
'Twas a piteous sight to see all around
The grain lie rotting on the ground.

Every day the starving poor
Crowded around Bishop Hatto's door,
For he had a plentiful last year's store ;
And all the neighborhood could tell
His granaries were furnished well.

At last Bishop Hatto appointed a day
To quiet the poor without delay :
He bade them to his great barn repair,
And they should have food for the winter there.

Rejoiced at such tidings good to hear,
The poor folk flocked from far and near :
The great barn was full as it could hold
Of women and children, and young and old.

The legend of Bishop Hatto in verse.

Then, when they saw it could hold no more,
Bishop Hatto he made fast the door ;
And while for mercy on Christ they call,
He set fire to the barn, and burned them all.

"I' faith 'tis an excellent bonfire !" quoth he,
"And the country is greatly obliged to me
For ridding it, in these times forlorn,
Of rats that only consume the corn."

So then to his palace returnéd he,
And he sat down to supper merrily,
And he slept that night like an innocent man ;
But Bishop Hatto never slept again.

In the morning, as he entered the hall
Where his picture hung against the wall,
A sweat like death all o'er him came,
For the rats had eaten it out of the frame.

As he looked there came a man from his farm ;
He had a countenance white with alarm.
"My lord, I opened your granaries this morn,
And the rats had eaten all your corn."

Another came running presently,
And he was pale as pale could be :
"Fly, my lord bishop, fly," quoth he ;
"Ten thousand rats are coming this way ;
The Lord forgive you for yesterday."

"I'll go to my tower on the Rhine," replied he
"'Tis the safest place in Germany ;
The walls are high, and the shores are steep,
And the stream is strong, and the water deep."

Bishop Hatto fearfully hastened away,
And he crossed the Rhine without delay,
And reached his tower, and barred with care
All the windows, doors, and loopholes there.

What Rollo and Minnie thought of the bishop's punishment.

He laid him down and closed his eyes ;
But soon a scream made him arise.
He started, and saw two eyes of flame
On his pillow, from whence the screaming came.

He listened and looked : it was only the cat :
But the bishop he grew more fearful for that ;
For she sat screaming, mad with fear
At the army of rats that were drawing near.

For they have swum over the river so deep,
And they have climbed the shores so steep,
And now by thousands up they crawl
To the holes and windows in the wall.

Down on his knees the bishop fell,
And faster and faster his beads did he tell,
As louder and louder, drawing near,
The saw of their teeth without he could hear.

And in at the windows, and in at the door,
And through the walls by thousands they pour,
And down through the ceiling and up through the floor,
From the right and the left, from behind and before,
From within and without, from above and below ;
And all at once at the bishop they go.

They have whetted their teeth against the stones,
And now they pick the bishop's bones ;
They gnawed the flesh from every limb,
For they were sent to do judgment on him.

"I'm glad they ate him up," said Minnie, as soon as Mr. George had finished reading the poetry. "I am very glad indeed."

"Yes," said Rollo, "so am I."

'What a pleasant ride this is!" said Rollo

after a little pause. It was, indeed, a delightful ride. The road was carried along the bank of the river a short distance above the level of the water. It was very hard, and smooth, and level; and on the side of it opposite to the water, the land rose abruptly in a steep ascent, which was covered with forest trees. At the distance of about a mile before them, down the river, they could see the towers and battlements of the castle which they were going to visit, rising among the tops of the trees, on a projecting promontory.

"I like the ride very much," said Rollo; "but I don't care much about the castle. I'm tired of castles."

"So am I," said Mr. George; "but this is different from the rest. This is a castle restored."

"What do you mean by that?" said Rollo.

"Why, nearly all the old castles on the Rhine," replied Mr. George, "have been abandoned, and have gone to decay; or else, if they have been repaired or rebuilt, they have been finished and furnished in the fashion of modern times. But this castle of Rheinstein, which we are now going to see, has been restored, as nearly as possible, to its ancient condition. The rooms, and the courts, and the towers, and battlements are all arranged as they used to be in former ages; and the furniture contained within is of the ancient fashion. The chairs, and tables, and cabinets, and all the other articles, are such as the barons used when the castles on the Rhine were inhabited."

"Where do they get such things nowadays?" asked Rollo.

"Some of the furniture which they have in this castle," said Mr. George, "originally belonged there, and has been kept there all the time, for hundreds of years. When they repaired and rebuilt the castle, they repaired this furniture too, and put it in perfect order. Some other furniture they bought from other old castles which the owners did not intend to repair, and some they had made new, after the ancient patterns. But here we are, close under the castle."

A few minutes after this, the carriage stopped in the road at the entrance to a broad, gravelled pathway, which diverged from the road directly under the castle walls, and began to ascend at once through the woods in zigzags. Mr. George and his party got out, and began to go up. The carriage, in the mean time, went on a few steps farther, to a smooth and level place by the roadside, under the shade of some trees, there to await the return of the party from their visit to the castle above.

"Now, children," said Mr. George, "we will see how you can stand hard climbing."

Rollo and Minnie looked up, and they could see the walls and battlements of the castle, resting upon and crowning the crags and precipices of the rock, far above their heads.

The road, or rather the pathway, — for it was not wide enough for a carriage, and was besides too steep, and turned too many sharp corners for wheels, — was very smooth and hard, and the children ascended it without any difficulty. They stopped frequently to look up, for at every turn there was some new view of the walls or battlements, or towers above, or of the crags and precipices of the rock on which the various constructions of masonry rested. The cliffs and precipices in many places overhung the path, and seemed ready to fall. In fact, in one place, an immense mass had cracked off, and was all ready to come down, but was retained in its place by a heavy iron chain, which passed around it, and was secured by clamps and staples to the more solid portion of the rock behind it. Rollo and Minnie looked up to this cliff, as they passed beneath it, with something like a feeling of terror.

"I should not like to have that rock come down upon our heads," said Minnie.

"No," said Rollo, " nor I ; but I should like to see it come down if we were out of the way."

At length the road, after many winding zig-zags and convolutions, came out upon a gravelled area in front of a great iron gate at an angle between two towers.

A man came from a courtyard within, and opened a small gate, which formed a part of the great one. He seemed to be a servant. Mr. George asked him in French if they could come in and see the castle. The man smiled and shook his head, but at the same time opened the loor wide, and stood on one side, as if to make way for them to come in.

" He says no," whispered Rollo.

" No," replied Mr. George, " his *no* means that he does not understand us ; but he wishes us to come in."

As Mr. George said these words, he passed through the gate, leading Minnie by the hand, and followed by Rollo.

The man shut the gate after them, and then began to say something to them, very fluently and earnestly, pointing at the same time to a door which opened upon a gallery that extended along the wall of a tower near by. As soon as ne had finished what seemed to be some sort of explanation, he left the party standing in the court, and returned to his work.

" He says," remarked Mr. George, " that there is a man coming to show us the castle."

" How do you know ? " asked Rollo.

" I know by the signs that he made," replied Mr. George. " Besides, I heard him say *schloss-vogt.*"

" What is *schloss-vogt ?* " asked Rollo.

" That was the ancient name for the officer who kept the keys of a castle," replied Mr. George, " and in restoring this castle they thought they would reëstablish the old office. So they call the man who keeps the keys the *schloss-vogt.*"

In a few minutes the *schloss-vogt* came. He was dressed in the ancient costume. He wore a black velvet frock coat, and green velvet cap, both made in a very antique and curious fashion, after the pattern of those worn, in ancient days, by the officers who had the custody of the keys in the baronial castles.

The *schloss-vogt* conducted his visitors all over the edifice that was under his charge. It would be impossible to describe the variety of halls, corridors, courts, towers, ramparts, and battlements which Rollo and Minnie were led to see. They went from one to another, until they were at length completely bewildered with the in tricacy, as well as dazzled by the magnificence, of the place. There were suites of most beautiful apartments, with polished floors, and painted walls, and furniture of the most curious and antique description. The chairs, the tables, the cabinets, and the beds of these rooms were all of the strangest forms ; and though they were of very elaborate and splendid workmanship, being richly carved and inlaid with mosaic work, and often ornamented with mountings of silver, they all wore a very antique and venerable air, which was extremely imposing. The rooms were of all shapes and sizes, and were arranged and connected with each other in the most odd and singular fashion, as the external walls which enclosed them were extremely irregular in plan, being conformed in a great measure to the shape of the rocks on which the castle was founded. The *schloss-vogt* was continually leading his party, as he guided them through the rooms, into some unexpected and curious place — a little cabinet, built on an angle of the wall ; a winding stair case, opening suddenly in a corner, and leading up to a watchtower, or down to a court ; a balcony overhanging a precipice, and commanding a most magnificent view up and down the river ; or some other curious nook or corner which in the snugness and coziness of its seclu sion, and the beauty of its adornments, filled the hearts of Rollo and Minnie with delight.

There were a great many specimens of ancient arms and armor, hung up in various halls in the castle, all of the most quaint and curious forms, but yet of the most elaborate and beautiful workmanship. There were swords, and daggers, and bows and arrows, and spurs, and shields, and coats of mail, and every other species of weapons, offensive and defensive, that the warriors of the middle ages were accustomed to use. Rollo was most interested in the bows and arrows. They were of great size, and were made in a style of workmanship, and ornamented with mountings and decorations, which Rollo had never dreamed of seeing in bows and arrows. Among the other articles of armor, the *schloss-vogt* showed the party a *gauntlet*, as it is called ; that is, an iron glove, which was worn in ancient times to defend the hand from the cuts of swords and sabres. The inside of the glove — I mean the part which covered the inside of the hand — was of leather ; but the back was formed of iron scales made to slide over each other, so as to allow the hand to open and shut freely, without making any opening in the iron. Mr. George tried this glove on, and so, in fact, did Rollo and Minnie. They were all surprised to find how well it fitted to the hand, and how freely the fingers could be moved while it was on. The *schloss-vogt* said that a man could write with it; and Mr. George placed his hand, with the glove upon it, in the proper position for writing, and then moved his fingers to and fro, as if there had been a pen between them.

" Yes," said he, " I think I could write with it very well."

All the furniture of the rooms was of a very quaint and curious description, while yet it was very rich and magnificent. There were elegant bedsteads of carved ebony surmounted with silken curtains and canopies of the most gorgeous description. There were cabinets inlaid with silver and pearl, and elegant cameos and mosaics, and a profusion of other such articles, all of which Rollo had very little time to examine, as the *schloss-vogt* led the party forward from one room to another without much delay.

The rooms themselves, in respect to form and arrangement, were almost as curious as the articles which they contained. Every one seemed different from the rest. You were constantly coming into the strangest and most unexpected places. There were cabinets, and wide halls, and intricate winding corridors, and open courts, and vaulted passages, and balconies, paved below and arched over above. At one place there was a light iron staircase built on the outside of a round tower, and as the tower itself was built on the pinnacle of an overhanging rock, you seemed, in ascending the staircase, to be poised in the air, with the rocks that lined the shore of the river beneath your feet, hundreds of feet below.

After rambling about the castle for half an hour, the party returned to the gate where they had come in, and the *schloss-vogt* bade them good by. He gave Minnie a little bouquet of flowers as she came away. They were flowers which he had gathered for her, one by one, from the plants growing in the various balconies, and in little parterres in the courtyards, which they passed in going about the castle. Minnie was very much pleased with this bouquet.

" I mean to press some of the flowers," said she, " and keep them for a souvenir."

" Yes," said Rollo, " I'll help you press them. I've got a pressing apparatus at home."

" Well," said Minnie, in a tone of great satisfaction. " And then, when they are pressed, I'll give you one of them."

So the party went down the zigzag path till they came to the main road at the bank of the river, and there getting into their carriage again, they rode home to the hotel.

CONCLUSION.

OUR travellers had now passed through all that portion of the Rhine which contains the castles and the romantic scenery. Above Bingen the valley of the Rhine widens ; that is, the mountains, instead of crowding in close to the river, recede from it many miles, enclosing a broad and level, but very fertile plain, through the midst of which the river flows between low banks, and with endless meanderings. The level country through which the river thus flows is inexpressibly beautiful, being divided into magnificent fields, and cultivated every where like a garden. It presents to the view a broad expanse of the richest verdure and beauty, but it cannot be seen from the steamboats on the river. Travellers are, accordingly, accustomed to leave the river at Mayence, a short distance above Bingen, and to go on up to Strasbourg by the railway. This was the plan which Mr. George and Rollo pursued.

From Strasbourg, Mr. George took passage for Paris by a railway train which left Strasbourg in the afternoon, so that they travelled all night. This was Rollo's plan. He wished to see how "it would seem," he said, to be travelling in the cars at midnight.

THE NIGHT JOURNEY.

He, however, fell asleep soon after dark, and slept soundly all the way.